Only the
Little Bone

Only the Little Bone

❖ ❖ ❖ ❖ ❖ ❖ ❖ ❖ ❖

STORIES BY

David Huddle

DAVID R. GODINE

Publisher · Boston

for my brothers,

CHARLES *and* BILL

First published in 1986 by
David R. Godine, Publisher, Inc.
Horticultural Hall
300 Massachusetts Avenue
Boston, Massachusetts 02115

Library of Congress Cataloging in Publication Data
Huddle, David, 1942–
    Only the little bone.
    Contents: Poison oak—Summer of the magic show—
The undesirable—[etc.]
    I. Title.
PS3558.U287O55   1986   813'.54   85-45962
ISBN 0-87923-774-0

First softcover printing 1988
Printed in the United States of America

Contents

Acknowledgments

For support, assistance, and encouragement in composing and revising these stories, the author is grateful to the National Endowment for the Arts, the University of Vermont, Yaddo, Mr. and Mrs. Joseph A. Massie, Jr., Lindsey Huddle, Charles Huddle, John Engels, Alan Broughton, Allen Shepherd, Margaret Edwards, Lyn Tisdale, and Dorothy Straight.

In slightly different form, "Poison Oak" and "Only the Little Bone" originally appeared in *New England Review / Bread Loaf Quarterly*, "Summer of the Magic Show" in *Grand Street*, "The Undesirable" in *Ploughshares*, "The Wedding Storm" in *Prairie Schooner*, "Save One for Mainz" in *Mid-American Review*, and "Dirge Notes" in *Colorado Quarterly*.

Only the
Little Bone

◆ ◆ ◆ ◆ ◆ ◆ ◆ ◆ ◆ ◆ ◆ ◆ ◆ ◆

Poison

Oak

Just before bedtime I slipped outside to stand for a while in the yard. I was afraid of the dark, and so I would not walk all the way around our house, but the side yard held shafts of light from the windows of my parents' bedroom and my father's study. I went along the edges of the lighted grass, then stood for what seemed like a long time. My father, at his desk, with his glasses tipped down to the end of his nose, held a stern expression on his face, but I knew he was kinder than he looked when he was working in his study.

On the ceiling upstairs I could see the moving shadows my mother made as she got ready to go to bed. I was not able to see her, but the shadows told me she was there, all right, in her nightgown, brushing her hair or putting cold cream on her face. Standing out on the damp grass, with cricket and frog noises all around, and looking into my own house, I imagined I had spun loose from my family.

Across the field at my grandparents' house, there was a light

3

on in their upstairs window, but it was too far away for me to see anyone inside. I walked a short distance out our driveway to a place where I could see all of the town that sat at the bottom of our hill. My grandmother said that the only pretty things about our town were its name, Rosemary, and how it looked at night from the top of our hill. Down there the streetlights shone like tiny beads on a string; the lighted house windows seemed to be blinking, though if I picked out any one of them and stared at it I could see that each one stayed steady. It was because those lights were so far away and so small that they seemed to be going on and off. I shivered, turned, and walked quickly back to our front porch.

When I came inside, I was breathing heavily, and I went to stand beside my father, who smelled like work and cigarettes. He would rather not have been disturbed by me then, but he put his hand on my rump and patted me gently. "Where've you been, Son?" he asked, and I told him, "Outside." He turned his head toward me to look at my face, trying to guess what I was thinking. But it was only a moment before he turned back to the book on his desk. I was glad to be able to stand there beside him, saying nothing at all, waiting for him to tell me to go upstairs to bed.

That summer my mother was teaching my brother and me to swim. We went to the New River, which ran below the back of our house, or else we drove to Elmo's Creek, where the trees made pleasant shaded places but where the water was colder, the current of it faster. I didn't think my mother enjoyed those swimming trips. My brother and I were fourteen and ten years old; we always misbehaved when we were together. And she was not an especially strong swimmer. But, perhaps because my father couldn't swim, my mother was determined that my brother and I learn how to get along in the water. She wanted us never to drown. When we got out of the car the three of us, pale in our bathing suits, were like people in a dream, walking down a dirt path, in patterns of light and shadow, toward the sound and smell of the moving water.

More than once we encountered drinkers. Around Rosemary, drinking men favored creek banks and river banks in warm weather. Some solitary ones would try to fish. Or there would be a loud group of five or six of them playing cards in a circle, sitting on rocks, old pieces of cardboard, big tin cans. A few of them came simply to sit staring at the water and drinking until they felt like going to sleep. The ones who fished or played cards did not trouble me, but I did not like coming upon a man lolled out flat on his back by the creek bank, his mouth open to the sun.

Such a sight frightened my mother, too—I had seen her flinch and go white in the face—but she would not be turned away. When we came upon those drinking men, we looked for a place to swim some distance away from them, but we took care not to seem to be running from them. My mother knew most of them by name anyway; some she had gone to school with, she said. Sometimes she spoke to them in a cordial way, but one that gave them to know she didn't approve of what they were doing. She was never treated disrespectfully.

My mother was married when she was very young, and people still considered her one of the prettiest women in Rosemary. Even wearing her old blue bathing suit, with a yellow towel over her shoulders, she could still draw herself up, toss her hair back, and suddenly look beautiful. I thought the reason my mother made those swimming trips, in spite of drinking men and paths where you could brush against poison oak or nearly step on a blacksnake lying in a patch of sun, was that she was proud of my brother and me. She could look straight through all our slapping and whining and giggling into what she thought we would become.

My grandfather had been superintendent of an iron-smelting furnace. My father had become the works manager of the carbide plant where Rosemary men worked in shifts twenty-four hours a day. I liked to go there at night to see the shadows of men walking around the great plumes of fire. One night, with all of us sitting in the car watching the men pouring huge vats of melted limestone and coke into molds, my mother turned around in the front seat to tell my brother and me solemnly, "Your father and grandfather have kept the town of Rosemary alive for the first half of the twentieth century."

My grandfather was retired, but he still employed a few men to look after his projects. He was a short man with a big nose and big ears and thick gold-rimmed spectacles. He wore khaki work clothes and a khaki hat. Every day he walked up through the apple trees, past the pigpen, to his toolshop, which was dark and cool as a cave. There he enjoyed having around him the men who were supposed to be working. Much of their day was spent sitting on boxes and benches swapping stories and making fun of each other. My grandfather's hair had fallen out when he was very young and had malaria; it had never come back. His face was a deep pink color—because he drank too much, my mother said. He called my grandmother "the old battle-ax." If Cassie came to cook for them in the afternoon, he liked to sit talking with her in the kitchen after quitting time, when his men had all gone back down the hill to their own houses.

The year before, Monkey Jones had quit, saying he could never work for us again, and Harvey Johnson had come to take his place. My grandfather accused Harvey of being a pretty man, and Harvey blushed whenever my grandfather said it. He was lean and very strong. The muscles of his arms and chest stood out under his skin. He had dark, wavy hair and a comb he kept in his back pocket. Harvey had tattoos on his arms and shoulders and hands. In the winter his skin was a pale milky color, but in the summer it turned dark brown. When you looked at Harvey's face, my mother said —because she sometimes found him watching her—it was hard to say what he was thinking. He couldn't read or write, but neither could Monkey Jones. My mother called him, jokingly, Cousin Harvey, because his last name was the same as her maiden name. She meant this joke to be generous, but she was, in a way, saying, How delightful it is that even though Harvey is who he is and I am who I am, we share a common name.

Harvey's main job was milking the four cows my grandmother insisted that my grandfather keep. Harvey lived in a house at the edge of the big field, halfway down the hill between the town and our house. The milk he took from the cows in the morning went to my grandparents, but in the evening he carried the big pail from the barn along the path across the field to our house. On our back porch my mother left him another pail and a clean piece of cheesecloth to strain the milk through when he poured it. Between milkings, Harvey was supposed to do odd chores for my grandfather, but my grandmother was actually the one who told him what to do.

My grandmother was very small and had a sharp face that seemed angry whenever she looked at anyone except my brother and me. She wore white dresses, white stockings, and black, lace-up shoes. She wore no underclothes, so that if she stood in front of a window you could see right through her dress. If she had a bruise on her leg or hip, she would hitch up her skirt and show it to you. Sometimes in the morning she stood at an upstairs window in a gauzy night-gown so worn that it didn't hide her breasts at all and shouted out angry instructions to my grandfather or one of his men. For a while I was embarrassed, but then I got used to her ways, as almost everyone who knew her did.

One of my grandfather's men always had to come to the house in the morning to cook for my grandmother. Harvey had to learn how she wanted her breakfast prepared; he had to have it ready for her just when she came downstairs. He was required to clean up the kitchen when she finished eating; he had to carry on with her the kind of talk that suited her at breakfast. Once I noticed him moving his lips silently while he stood at the sink washing her dishes with his back to her. My grandmother was rarely cheerful. Over the years, she said, she had found that for her morning mood men were better than women. Later in the day, Harvey had housecleaning chores, or else yard duties.

In the summer, my grandmother followed her yard man around from rosebush to apple tree to lilac bush, giving him a constant flow of instruction and criticism. The vegetable garden had to be tended in a certain way. My grandmother believed in organic gardening; she worried about compost, though to each other the men who worked for my grandfather made jokes about it. Bugs that could have been dusted or sprayed had to be picked off by hand and dropped in tin cans with a little kerosene in them.

In the winter, things were probably easier for Harvey; tending the big coal furnace was something he could do in the basement without my grandmother watching him. And in the winter she demanded less conversation. Cold weather convinced her she was right in her opinions, most of which had to do with people going to the dogs and with what President Roosevelt had done years ago. Sipping her tea, staring out her kitchen window at the scruffy winter landscape, my grandmother wanted no more than an occasional *yes ma'am* from Harvey.

He could pick me up and toss me around like a small sack

of cattle feed. He teased me about my glasses, my big forehead, the words I used, and the questions I asked him. He
liked to suggest to my brother and me, while we stood watching him milk in the manure-smelling barn, the things that
women and men did with each other that my brother and I
ought to know about. "You're pretty smart," he said, "but
you don't know everything, do you?" When we asked him to
tell us, he sighed, pretending that our ignorance made him
sad, and said, "I reckon you'll find out in plenty of time."
Or else he punched our chests with his big fingers and told
us to get the hell home. If we climbed up to the barn roof
to stomp on it while he was trying to milk, he came out and
threw corncobs or chunks of dried cow manure at us. If we
sneaked behind him to try to scare him, he chased us and
threatened to lock us up in the little toolshed behind the barn.
"No one will ever find you," he said, "and your family will
forget all about you."

Harvey told us about his tattoos, where he got them, what
they meant. My favorite was the one on his arm, half fish
and half woman; he could make her dance by squeezing
his muscle.

Harvey held chickens up by the feet, with their heads laid
across the chopping block; he let Duncan and me cut their
heads off with the ax. He laughed at us if we did not make
a clean cut; he laughed when he threw the headless, flapping
bodies in the dirt where they jumped and lurched and sprayed
blood on the weeds. He demonstrated for us how he rolled
his own cigarettes, let us take the can of Prince Albert tobacco
and hold it under our noses. Once he even let my brother
lick the cigarette paper, but Duncan made a face and spat
after he did it. He talked about hunting and fishing with his
old daddy. He asked about our swimming lessons, about whether
or not we wore swimming suits. He liked to remind us of

how he was taught, his daddy throwing him, naked, out into the deep part of the river and yelling, "Now swim, goddamn you!"

It took me longer to learn how to do it than it did my brother, of whom my mother began saying, "Duncan is a powerful swimmer." I remained clumsy, but I could swim. I wouldn't drown.

My mother said that she hated the thought of our getting too grown up for her to take us to the quiet beauty of our swimming places. Of course anyone could see that she was wrong, that those places had been cluttered with all kinds of trash. The river water was always a dirty brown color. I knew that raw sewage was dumped in it from small industrial plants in towns like Rosemary all along the river, from factories like my father's carbide plant. We had to watch out for broken glass on the bottom of Elmo's Creek. Trees had been hacked down to make firewood for drinkers and card-players. There were human turds on the paths that went from the road to the water. Those places weren't pretty at all, but then my mother saw things as she thought they ought to be. Once or twice she tried driving us to the chlorinated waters of the public swimming pool in Madison, twenty miles from our town, but we were not comfortable in that crowd of swimmers who were strangers to us.

That August my mother began to be troubled by poison oak. It was at the edges of the yard, in the honeysuckle on the fence, along the dirt-and-gravel driveway, on the path across the field to my grandparents' house. The blisters came on her hands and arms and feet and ankles. It was hard for her not to scratch and make the blisters worse. She used calamine lotion, which dried in pink smudges and had a smell that I didn't like. Her blisters did not heal in ordinary time. On hot days she went upstairs and lay down. She said she felt half sick all day. My grandfather sent Harvey Johnson and Earl Sexton over to our house to spray. The spray killed all the weeds and vines it touched. Around our yard there was a boundary of brown, dead stuff. The spraying did not help my mother. She couldn't take us on swimming trips anymore because the river and creek banks were places where poison oak grew freely.

When I told Harvey that I was not exactly certain what poison oak looked like, he took me to the pile of warped lumber that lay stacked up against the side of the barn. I did not like that place because my brother said that he'd seen a copperhead there, lying on one of those gray boards. My grandfather said that it was most unlikely the snake was a copperhead, that probably what Duncan had seen was a large night crawler. Harvey and I went along the edge of the lumber pile until he saw what he was looking for, a weed with three shiny leaves at the end of each of its little branches. He squatted down beside the weed, then put his hand under the leaves, as if he were showing me a flower. He didn't say anything, but I knew he meant to tell me that this was poison oak. "Won't you get it?" I asked him. Still he said nothing, but with his fingers, delicately, he pinched off a clump of leaves. He held it a moment in his hand; then he crumpled and rolled the leaves between both his hands. For a moment he looked at the little wadded-up wafer of green stuff in the palm of his hand. Then he lifted it up to his mouth, put it in, and swallowed, all the while grinning steadily at me. "You'll die, won't you?" I asked him. He shook his head, holding his mouth as if he were chewing tobacco.

One morning just before school started, I was going to town with my mother for groceries. She had been short-tempered and angry all morning because the poison oak had gotten onto her in a very bad way. It was on her thighs and hips now, and the calamine lotion didn't help to take away the itching. All morning she had been about to cry. When she was like that, I got nervous. I wanted her to be nice to me. I wanted to be pleasing to her, to make her laugh. So I hovered too close to her, talking too much and too loudly; then, when she fussed at me, I complained and whined. She threatened to leave me at home by myself, but I knew she didn't want to do that.

When we got into the car, it was not easy for my mother to sit comfortably on the seat. She tried arranging her dress under her in several ways, but all of them were wrong. Finally she pulled the dress up behind her so that she sat on the seat with only her bare legs and her underwear. The dress covered her lap and the tops of her legs, but it left open for me to see a space of blistered skin on her thighs and hips and rump. I did not like her to drive in the car that way.

At first I was quiet, because I could tell she was uncomfortable and again about to cry. When she was like that, she wasn't beautiful at all; her face became the wrong color, pinched, and damp-looking. We drove down the hill into town, and when she stopped the car at Mrs. Elkins's store, I was crying directly at her. "What's wrong?" she asked, but I couldn't tell her. "Big boy like you, crying this way!" she said. Finally she said that I had to stay in the car if I was going to keep acting that way. And she got out. When she stepped onto the dirt parking lot in front of the store, her dress fell immediately down over her legs. She was properly covered again. There were no people outside the store to have seen her, but I felt that all the men of our town had seen my mother's blistered skin, and I kept crying.

That fall and winter my parents discussed something that my brother and I were not allowed to hear very much about. Something was wrong, our parents were concerned about it, but we could feel only that they were troubled, that they did not wish us to know what it was, and that perhaps they were afraid of it.

In the spring, however, we began to know what was wrong: someone was coming into our house when we were out. They did not steal, or, if they stole, they took only things that were not important. But they left traces of having been there. My brother and I did not know what those traces were, but our parents saw things that told them someone had been inside the house. Things were done in my parents' bedroom.

In the top drawer of his bureau, my father kept a small pistol, a black one with a cylinder of small copper cartridges. Once I went to the dresser, opened the drawer, and looked at the pistol. Another time I took it in my hand and held it a few moments before carefully putting it back. This drawer of my father's bureau had a secret smell when it was opened. I could imagine someone opening that drawer, breathing in that smell, taking out the pistol and pointing it. I savored this vision much of the time I was daydreaming in school; with it I was able to give myself wonderful jolts of fear at night when I buried myself down in the bedcovers.

In late spring, when the drive-in theater opened up at Gantley, we planned, long in advance, a trip to see a John Wayne movie. My mother enjoyed talking with my father about John Wayne. She said that he managed to hurt himself in every movie. For a week, each night at supper our parents brought up the subject of the movie. Duncan and I were surprised they were so interested in it, but we were happy to talk with them about it.

When the evening came, we left home sooner than we usually did, and my father turned the car in the wrong direction when we left our driveway. As he drove, my father explained that we were actually going to the deputy sheriff's to pick him up, then drive him back to our place, where he would wait to catch the person who had been coming into our house.

My brother and I became quiet while we were waiting outside Alan Hudson's house. He was the only law officer within twelve miles of Rosemary. He had a reputation of being more than willing to fight anyone who wanted to try him out. When he climbed into our car, he was polite to my mother and father, but he paid little attention to my brother or me. His uniform was dark blue with glittering buttons, with a pistol—much larger than my father's—and a thin black club that dangled at his hip from a leather thong.

When we turned back into our driveway, the deputy ducked down beside me into the floor-space behind the front seat. Duncan was sitting up front with my mother and father, so that he had to squirm to get a look at Alan Hudson. I knew he wished he could trade places with me to be where I sat staring at the huge man hunkered down in the seat beside me. My father stopped the car beside the small shack that held our kindling and firewood. Alan Hudson slid out of the car and into the shadows of the woodshed while my mother got out and went into our house, pretending to get something we had gone off and forgotten. Then we made the circle around our garage and back out the driveway. Riding on the winding road through the mountains to Gantley, my brother and I questioned our parents about the trap they had set up. My brother asked why they had not told us of their plan, but they did not give him an answer; instead, while we were watching them, they smiled at each other.

The movie was *The Quiet Man*. It was about Ireland, where John Wayne was the quiet man who was in love with the red-haired woman, Maureen O'Hara, who was beautiful when she became angry and shouted at all the men. John Wayne fought a great deal. Once he and another man fell into a river while they were fighting, and he hurt himself so that he had to limp and carry his arm in a sling. I thought of Alan Hudson back at our house, and I shivered to myself in my corner of the car when I imagined Alan Hudson, perhaps right at that moment, fighting with our intruder in my parents' bedroom, rolling across the bed as men in the movie rolled across the tables and floors. The noise of their fists hitting each other was loud.

But when we returned home, Alan Hudson was standing in the driveway, smoking a cigarette in the dark. No one had come the whole time we were gone. He apologized to my parents for not having caught our intruder; my parents apologized to him for having kept him out late for nothing. He told them that a cow had come up to the shed and frightened him; they all three laughed politely. Alan Hudson stomped out his cigarette before he got into our car for my father to drive him home. My mother took my brother and me into our house and sent us upstairs to bed while she waited for my father to come back. She seemed tired and sad then, though at the movie she had laughed with all of us and had let her head rest against my father's shoulder.

Harvey's wife was a large woman named Janice whose face was puffy like dough and who always called me Honey whenever she spoke to me. Harvey had a son named Billy who was small and mean and strong for his age. Billy was younger than my brother and me, but we would not play with him because he usually ended up wanting to fight with us. Harvey had a daughter named Loretta whose face was broad and ready to smile, who that year had developed breasts, whose voice was always a little too loud. I walked down the hill past Harvey's house when I went to school in the morning, when there was smoke coming from the chimney that went down into their kitchen. I walked past it again when I was coming home in the afternoon, and then the sunlight was usually slanting into the hill, making a long shadow of Harvey's house up into the field that was my grandfather's pasture land.

At school George Clemons had shown me a sign that you could make to a girl to invite her to screw with you. You made the sign by holding up the little finger and forefinger of your hand. When you made the sign, the girl would know what you wanted, and she would let you know whether or not she was interested. George explained to me that it was a sort of code that everyone except me had known for a long time. I didn't trust George because I knew he resented my being the smartest one in our class. But I was desperate to find out about what he was telling me. I wasn't certain exactly what was involved in it, but George explained it to me in such a way that I imagined I could do it. George told me that it was easy and that I would be glad when I had done it. "You might have to take off your glasses," he advised me.

I made a plan for giving the sign to Loretta. She was not exactly the girl I would have chosen to invite, but I saw her often, and she was always friendly toward me. I had a vague longing for something, and as George had described screwing to me, I expected it was screwing that I wanted without really knowing it.

I found a good place deep down in the pasture between our house and Harvey's house. It was a small clearing among the scrub cedars that grew there. Several afternoons I picked broomsage and lined the clearing with it until it became comfortable to sit or lie down there.

Usually when I was coming home from school there was no one outside on Harvey's porch. Certainly I could not go knock on the door of their house and make the sign to Loretta

when she came to answer it. One day Loretta was sitting out
on the steps near the kitchen door, but Janice, cumbersome
and doughy-armed, was hanging up clothes on the line stretched
post to post on the back porch. "Hello, Honey," said Janice.
"Hello, Brain," Loretta called out to me. She meant to be
joking with me, but I did not like being called that name. I
couldn't help knowing what I knew at school. I began to think
I would not have a chance to make the sign to Loretta before
school was out, and after that I would have no good excuse
for walking past her house.

Finally, though, on a sunny day when smoke was lying in
soft white layers over the whole town, I walked past Harvey's
house, and Loretta was again sitting on the steps of her back
porch. She sang out her greeting to me, and Harvey and
Janice and Billy were not around. I spoke to her, but I was
very nervous. I kept walking up the hill toward my house.

Just as I was about to go through the rickety gate up into
the pasture, I made myself turn and give the sign to Loretta.
I did it very clearly so that there could be no mistake about
my invitation. Loretta seemed startled by what I had done
and for a moment sat perfectly still, staring at me as I held
my hand up into the air in front of me. Then she sang out,
"Same to you."

I was not prepared for that response. I could only think to
say, "Do you want to?" I felt giddy in the afternoon sunlight.
For weeks at school I had daydreamed of Loretta and me
strolling up through the pasture until we came to the clearing
I had arranged for us among the cedar trees.

"Want to what?" she called out to me, very pleasantly, as
if this were all teasing.

I knew then that George had misguided me, but I was
stunned with what I couldn't say. I turned my back to her
and passed quickly through the gate, going up the path to my

house. "I don't know," I said back over my shoulder, but I was pretty sure I had not said it loud enough for her to hear me. "I don't know," I said again, but even that second time I didn't say it loud enough.

Saturday afternoon, the last weekend before school was out, Harvey stood outside our screen door telling my mother that some boys had turned a boat over in the river. He was not certain who they were, but he thought they were Cassie's twins—Cassie who cooked for my grandparents. They were my classmates. Harvey walked down the hill from our house toward the river.

Soon my mother and my father and my brother and I walked down the hill that way, too. People from town were walking in one direction on the river road; we followed them. Some of the women were crying. There was a white County Rescue Squad truck parked where most of the people had stopped walking and now stood in groups, murmuring, looking out toward the wide surface of moving brown water.

There were two boats out there with men in them. The men were holding onto ropes that went down into the water. Soon we heard voices raised in one boat; then they began pulling the ropes up. They pulled a boy my size up out of the water. It was Pete, one of Cassie's twins. He was wearing overalls and a shirt the blue color that the men of our town wore. He was heavy with water, so that it took them a long time, but when they had him in the boat they sped up the outboard motor and glided quickly in to the bank.

My mother went to see about Pete. My father stayed with Duncan and me, a short distance away from the white truck. We did not say anything. Soon they found L. C., the other twin; they pulled him up out of the water, too, and brought him in to the bank. My mother was there seeing about them.

I heard her voice, much too high, saying something that was both insistent and a question: "Can't you make them live?" But then I did not hear her anymore, and soon she came back to us.

We walked home. When my mother stumbled on a railroad tie, her toe began to bleed. My father helped her walk. My brother and I walked apart from them and from each other.

After the twins drowned, I was the same, but my mother had changed. She decided to make certain Duncan and I could swim. My father wasn't happy with that; he said she'd seen us both swim before. He asked her if she wanted to spend another summer with poison oak on her. She said that she knew what she had to do and that she was perfectly capable of watching out for poison oak because she had had plenty of experience with it.

So we went on another swimming trip. We drove to Elmo's Creek on a clear, warm day. My mother began singing in the car when we turned onto the creek road. My brother said aloud what I was already thinking: "Mother, please don't sing." My mother went on singing as if she hadn't heard him. She parked the car, and we got out, the three of us again in a dream, padding along the dirt path toward the water, my mother holding my hand even though I was wishing she wouldn't.

When we reached the creek, my mother began gathering beer cans that had been dropped all around the swimming place. She told us to go ahead into the water while she finished what she was doing. She told us to enjoy ourselves and to forget that she was there with us. She sang.

My brother went first, but I quickly followed him. He dove out into the deep water and swam a few strokes. Then he stopped and began splashing water at me. I squatted down into the water, which was so cold it made my whole body ripple on my bones. I pretended to swim a little, but I knew the creek bottom was just underneath my body; if I wanted to, I could stand up and the water would be no deeper than up to my chest. My brother kept splashing me. Soon I was with him, splashing, shouting, running in and out of the water. It was fun to play that way, but I did not go out into the deep part. I made sure my mother saw me making swimming strokes, though it was actually only pretending to swim because I knew I was not in the deep water.

My mother finished gathering the beer cans. She waded out a little distance into the water, but she didn't come in far enough even to get her bathing suit wet. She smiled at us and walked back out onto the creek bank, found a place in the sunlight to put down her towel and lie on it. She closed her eyes, with her face turned toward us, but I believed she was still watching us through slitted eyelids, merely pretending to close her eyes.

Duncan and I came out of the water and stripped off our bathing suits to put on our dry clothes. My brother had hair where I had only pale skin. My mother went away from us a short distance to change her clothes, too, even though her bathing suit was not wet. We strolled along the path back toward the car, all three of us carrying the old cans she had gathered, using our towels for sacks.

Then my mother was in bed all day. Dr. Williams came to see her in the morning and again in the evening. Her door was always closed. Sometimes when I walked quietly past it, I could hear her crying in there. She had poison oak again. This time it was not the same. I heard my father talking to Dr. Williams out on the porch. He said, "She has it nowhere on her whole body except where that swimming suit touched her. The only way that could have happened was if somebody rubbed that stuff into the inside of the swimming suit. I want you to tell me, what kind of a son of a bitch would do that?" — *)ead one to believe Harvy did it?*

No one cooked my grandmother's breakfast for a little while, but then Monkey Jones came up on the hill to work for us again, and he was the one who talked with my grandmother each morning. He helped her clean house. He did her yardwork for her. My grandmother complained that he wasn't any better at working for her now than he used to be. Monkey Jones had done this same work before, but after a while he'd taken to drinking in the morning, coming to work surly, unshaven, and bad-smelling. My grandmother had yelled at him almost every day, so that finally he'd quit. My grandmother said she had fired him.

But now he had been saved at the Church of God, and he had changed. Now he felt that God would help him and my grandmother to get along better. Now he did the milking and carried the milk to our house where he strained it through the clean cheesecloth into our pail.

Monkey was called Monkey by everyone in Rosemary, even by my mother. He had a square face with a short forehead and tiny eyes spaced wide apart. His skin was leathery. His having no teeth gave his mouth a funny, loose kind of pursed look. His arms were too long for the rest of his body. Monkey had eight children, but only one of them was right, my grandfather said.

My grandmother wished Harvey were still working for us. I could tell that, even though she never mentioned his name. At supper one night, I had told about the time Harvey ate the poison oak, and no one talked about him after that. He and Janice and Billy and Loretta were gone; their house was empty, and our parents wouldn't let Duncan and me talk about them either.

Now when Monkey Jones talked with me, he told me how much he admired my grandmother. He said, "That day your grandmother yelled at me from the window, before she'd even gotten her clothes on that morning, and she cursed me and called me every kind of name because I didn't snap those beans the way she wanted done—I don't think about that day. It's like I don't even remember it at all." Monkey was like my mother that way; there were some things he chose not to know.

Monkey called both me and my brother Honey, and it made Duncan mad because he felt he was too old for such a name. I liked Monkey because he was very nice to me; he said that I was the smartest boy my age that he had ever met. I was flattered, of course, by what he said about me, but I was becoming less and less interested in him. The only time he seemed at all dangerous was when he went into the barn to pray after he ate his lunch out of his dinner-bucket. We could hear him in there by himself praying at the top of his voice for a long time. The voice that shouted those prayers up into the dust-filled air of the barn was frantic, high-pitched, so urgent that I could imagine Monkey Jones clinging to the edge of a cliff and begging someone to take him by the hand and pull him up to where it was safe.

One day when he had finished milking and I was walking with him toward our house to deliver our milk, I asked him what he prayed about. Then his voice was serene. He told me he prayed for every man, woman, and child in Rosemary. He prayed for the twins, Pete and L. C., whom the Lord saw fit to take away from us while they were still so young and innocent. He prayed for my mother to be healed of the terrible affliction that had troubled her all summer. He prayed for my grandmother, and he prayed for me. I asked him what he prayed to happen to me, and he thought a long time before he answered.

Finally he said that he prayed for me that I would be able to use my mind to do the Lord's work and that I would grow up walking the path of righteousness. I thanked Monkey for praying for me and for all my family in such a kind way, and then, though it was mean of me, perhaps, to ask this of him, I asked him anyway, "Is the path of righteousness anything like this one here we're walking on, Monkey?" It was a path through the high grass and broomsage and weeds of every kind. But Monkey understood at least part of the joke I was making and said, "Lord God, Honey, I guess it is. Lord God."

Harvy-obsession with mother (most beautiful)
   - poison oak + thief
  - mother: says they share a common name.
- narrator doesn't know who did it
  -gives bits + pieces of info.

Summer of

the Magic Show

One October night in his second year at the University of Virginia, my brother persuaded a young woman to drive him to a scenic overlook at the top of Afton Mountain. They sat in the dark car a few moments, but they didn't talk. The young woman lit a cigarette just before they both climbed out. There were no stars, no moon, no street or house or car lights.

And they stayed quiet. The woman leaned against her car's front fender, crossed one arm in front of her, held the cigarette near her face, and kept her eyes on Duncan.

It was so dark, Duncan says, he could step away from her only a pace and a half and still see her face and her blond hair. He took a white handkerchief from his jacket pocket— U. Va. students wore coats and ties then—shook the folds out, and held it at arm's length from himself.

A rifle-shot went off not ten yards from them, so loud that Duncan, who knew it was coming, says he couldn't help flinching. The young woman yelped, crouched, dropped her cigarette, crossed her arms in front of her face to protect herself. Duncan had been too startled to notice if the handkerchief had flapped or not, but it had the bullet hole through it, and he carried it over to show to the young woman. He made the desired impression on her: that night so frightened her that she moved away from Charlottesville, where she'd lived most of her life.

Duncan says he regrets what he did. He had arranged for his friend Bobby Langston to wait with his squirrel-rifle up there on the Skyline Drive, and he was lucky Bobby had his night vision and was such an accurate shot as to be able to hit that handkerchief, dark as it was. With the shot, Duncan stopped wanting to harm the woman, but by then, of course, he had already done it. I regret knowing the story and what it tells about him.

Back when he was fourteen, Duncan was taller than anybody in our town—six-five—and thin, but very strong. No matter how much needling he took from the coaches over at Madison High School, he wouldn't play basketball or football for them. Duncan was an intellectual, and he was an innocent boy. He was pale and hairy, wore glasses, was not what anybody'd call handsome. He never really had a date until his senior year of high school.

He was the smartest one ever to come out of our town. No one begrudged him his brains, though my father often shook his head over what he called "the ways Duncan chooses to put his intelligence to use." Duncan's passion was magic. When he was thirteen he found an old *Tarbell Correspondence Course for the Apprentice Magician* in my grandparents' attic, and he read through the year's worth of lessons in about a week.

He put on his first magic show, in our living room, for

Uncle Jack and Aunt Mary Alice. I remember that he messed up the Mystical Multiplying Balls, dropped one of the hollow shells right in the middle of his audience and had to stoop, humiliatingly, and pick it up. But he went on, and when he finished the show my parents and aunt and uncle applauded. What else could they do? They didn't know it was going to have a permanent effect on him.

Duncan went on doing tricks for the kids on the bus, who thought he was a freak, and for the kids in his homeroom, who were happy to have him pass the time for them, and so on, until finally Mrs. Pug Jones promised him five dollars if he'd come to Buntsy's birthday party and keep the kids from tearing her house apart. When he came back from Buntsy's party, Duncan showed me the five-dollar bill and said that now he was a professional.

The time I was closest to Duncan was the summer between his first and second years in engineering school at the University of Virginia. He was a National Merit Scholar, the only one we'd had from our whole county. He'd gotten a summer job running the scales for Pendleton over at the rock quarry, and he'd decided to put on a magic show for the town of Rosemary. He told us his plans and started working on us at the supper Mother fixed to celebrate his homecoming from Charlottesville. He wanted my mother to get the Ladies' Aid to sponsor him and my father to talk to the Superintendent of Schools to get him the use of the auditorium. My mother was still a little intoxicated from seeing the Lawn and the Rotunda at the University of Virginia when she drove up there to get him. My father gave Duncan his old slow shake of the head, but he didn't say no. It was a supper where Duncan did all the talking anyway, which was his right, having managed not to flunk out of school like everybody else from Rosemary who went away to college. The plans he told us about for the show were modest ones, a lot of card tricks and sleight-of-hand stuff he'd been practicing for his roommate, Will Greenwood. My father and I packed in the steak and mashed potatoes and peas that were Duncan's celebration supper, and my mother listened to his newly sophisticated talk, hardly touching what was on her plate.

Duncan just assumed I'd help him with the magic show, but that didn't bother me. I had nothing else to do that summer except mow yards for the three or four people in town who wanted them mowed. Rosemary probably had more houses in it that were surrounded by packed-down dirt, with chickens pecking in the dust and dogs under the porch, than it had houses with grass around them. Even the people who were willing to pay me to cut their grass were doing me a favor. So was Duncan, who pronounced me his "stage manager and first assistant."

The more Duncan thought about it—mostly while he was wearing a hard hat and making check-marks on a clipboard over at the rock quarry—the more he realized card tricks and sleight-of-hand wouldn't be good enough for his show. We had to have more illusions, a Chinese Disappearing Cabinet, a Flaming Omelet Bowl that changed the fire into dozens of silk scarves and then changed them into two white doves, a Guillotined Girl, and a Floating Lady. He talked my grandfather into helping him weld together an elaborate device of heavy pipes that he needed for the Floating Lady. He set me to work building, according to diagrams he drew, the Chinese Cabinet. He saw Toots Polk down at the post office one morning, and he persuaded her to be his Guillotined Girl. While he was at it, he asked her if she wouldn't mind doing a few of her dance numbers.

He decided I'd do a couple of trumpet solos, too, just to balance out Toots's tap-dancing. I'd gotten to be pretty good at "It's Cherry Pink and Apple Blossom White." Duncan said I could do that one and one more. I chose "Tammy," which in my opinion I played with a great deal of feeling.

On weekends when Duncan didn't have to work for Pendleton, he and I spent most of the day in the empty schoolhouse, building and painting flats for the set, working on the lighting, blocking out the show. There was a battered upright school piano in there, below and to the right of the stage. I plunked around on that when things got slow. Duncan always asked me to play one of the two songs he liked to sing, "Old Man River" and "Unchained Melody." He stood at center stage and bellowed out the words at the top of his voice, but he held himself formally, as if he had on white tie and tails. At least once every time he and I were in there alone, he had a go at "Unchained Melody."

Duncan had been getting letters from Charlottesville, and he'd mentioned a woman's name in connection with the theater group for which he had done some lighting work. So it wasn't quite a surprise when he announced that Susan O'Meara would be visiting us for a week at the beginning of July.

Susan was twenty-two. Duncan was eighteen. She smoked and wore jeans, men's shirts untucked, and no makeup; what her blond hair looked like didn't seem to matter to her. She drove up to our house one afternoon in a beat-up white Ford. She got there before Duncan had come home from the rock quarry, and right off she told Mother that it was so damn hot in that car, could she please take a bath? I couldn't remember when a woman had ever said *damn* in front of my mother; it startled me to have a strange woman come into our house and go straight upstairs to take a bath. I waited for a sign from Mother, but she remained calm. I was dumbfounded at supper that evening, halfway through my first piece of fried chicken, when I looked and saw, first, that Susan O'Meara was cutting hers with a knife and fork, and then that Mother and Duncan were doing the same with theirs. My father and I stuck to our usual method, but neither of us went beyond our second piece.

Susan talked about the heat in Charlottesville, about her father, who was a doctor, about her mother, who taught biology at St. Ann's. Susan said *damn* again during the meal; then during dessert she laughed and said she had recently told David Weiss of the Virginia Players to go to hell.

I figured my mother was bound to correct that kind of talk at her supper table, but they all went on eating their berry pie, and I was the only one who drowned his in sugar and milk—my mother had given my father a look when he reached for the cream pitcher.

Duncan, for once, wasn't saying much, but he sure was listening to every word Susan spoke. Finally the two of them excused themselves and left the house to go to the drive-in. When I stepped to the window to see which one of them was going to drive, Mother snapped at me to stop spying on them. I saw Duncan open the door of her Ford and Susan climb in on the driver's side.

I waited around the table hoping to hear some interesting opinions of Susan from one or the other of my parents, but they offered nothing. My father did have seconds on the berry pie, and this time he treated himself to plenty of sugar and milk. I asked them straight out, "What do you think of her?"

It was one of the most reasonable questions I'd ever asked them, but I didn't get an answer. What I did get was a look from each of them, neither of which I understood. Then they gave each other another look, and I didn't understand that either.

On the weekend Susan, in her jeans and a sweatshirt, worked over at the schoolhouse with Duncan and me. Mostly she sat in the second row, dangling her feet over the wooden back of the seat in front of her, smoking, and offering suggestions to Duncan. Anything I had to say he had always only half-listened to, but he took notes when Susan told him something. Once she climbed up on a ladder to examine some of the lights above the stage. For a long while she shouted down remarks for Duncan, who stood holding the ladder and gazing up at her.

She wasn't rude to me or to my father, but she dealt with us as if we were photographs of Duncan's cute little brother and his old codger of a father. She never asked us questions the way she sometimes did Mother.

On the last evening she spent with us, Susan wore this little diamond ring Duncan had bought her with his Pendleton money. It couldn't have been anything but the smallest stone they had at Smith's Jewelers, but it probably cost Duncan every cent he had in his savings account at the time. I wouldn't have noticed it if I hadn't caught Mother with her eye on it during the meal.

Obviously Duncan and Susan meant for the rest of us to understand that they were engaged, but for some reason neither of them said anything aloud about it. My father and I weren't about to say anything on our own, and so it was up to my mother to mention it if anybody was going to, and she chose not to. It was as if since nobody gave voice to it, the engagement hadn't really come about. There was the ring on Susan's finger—she chewed her nails, by the way—but without any words being spoken there was no engagement. That last night I did notice a way Susan had of widening her eyes when she talked that made me understand just for an instant what Duncan saw in her, "one of the most brilliant minds in Albemarle County," as he put it.

Next morning, to see her leave, I snuck out of bed and

knelt by the window. It was early because Duncan had to go to work at the quarry. My mother and Duncan and Susan all came out to the car together. Mother gave Susan a sort of official kiss on the cheek, so measured that I imagined she must have thought about it all through their breakfast, and Susan had to hold her cigarette away from Mother with her free hand. Then Mother went back inside, Susan stamped out her cigarette in our driveway, and she and Duncan went into this farewell embrace and kiss. I was surprised at how embarrassed I felt to be seeing it, though I confess it was exactly what I had come to the window to see. Maybe I thought it was going to be funny or sexy, but it was neither of those, and I can't really say what it was. When Susan climbed in behind the steering wheel, Duncan leaned in to kiss her goodbye again. And when she was gone, with the dust from her car still hanging above the driveway, Duncan stood out there alone with his hands in his pockets, toeing at something on the ground. I noticed then how skinny he was, how the sun had burnt his neck and arms.

This was the same morning my mother decided, as she put it, "to inaugurate a custom for the good of our family." She meant to correct the social behavior of my father and me, who had not gracefully carried off Susan O'Meara's visit. Mother didn't ask us what we thought about it, and we knew from her tone of voice not to argue. She commissioned me to ask a girl to our house for my birthday supper. Every birthday, she said, a girl should be invited.

To put it in straightforward terms, girls made my father uncomfortable. Susan O'Meara had come close to paralyzing him. He was a courtly man. When we sat in the dining room, which was when we had company, he stood and held my mother's chair for her until she came in to sit down. He spoke with elaborate courtesy to all the women on my mother's side of the family and said *yes ma'am* and *no ma'am* to most of them. In fact, I felt that in the presence of women, my mother excepted, my father was never himself. He limited his conversation to expressing agreement with the people around him or to asking questions of them. If questioned himself, he phrased his replies in such a way as to generalize or abstract whatever he was telling, so that his opinions in this voice were dull, his experiences hardly worth mentioning. My father was a man who had faced an old toolshed full of rattlesnakes, had been shot at by union strikers, had taken a knife away from Bernard Seeger at a high-school dance, but around women who came to our house as company, and especially around Susan O'Meara that past week, my father took on the personality of somebody who'd stayed indoors all his life and eaten nothing but cheese sandwiches.

I didn't resent my mother's decision, as perhaps I might have any other summer. I had noticed that my parents treated Duncan like a grownup while Susan was in the house; I knew a girl who was almost as formidable as Susan: Jean Sharp. She was from Palm Beach, Florida. Even though she was only thirteen, I'd heard her say things that showed she thought Rosemary, Virginia, was far back in the wilderness.

I was Jean's grandmother's yard-boy. When I finished mowing her yard, old Mrs. Sharp had me come inside for lemonade before she paid me. While I stood there, sweating in her kitchen, she coaxed some conversation out of me, then some out of Jean standing in the kitchen doorway. Jean had very fine dark hair, a small nose and mouth, a lanky frame. When Jean and I gave the appearance of being able to talk with each other, Mrs. Sharp handed me the money and suggested that we go into the living room and play cards. Jean taught me cribbage while sitting forward on the sofa with her back very straight, her knees bent and together, her ankles crossed. All that summer Jean had worn sundresses; they emphasized her flat-chestedness, but there was something about her in those dresses, her thin shoulders maybe, that was sexy. Her fingers playing the cards or moving the pegs on the cribbage board held my attention. Her soft voice, her precise diction, made me feel I was learning something every time she spoke to me.

My father had seen Jean only a few times in all her summers of visiting her grandmother in Rosemary, but he knew about her. When my mother and I talked it through to the conclusion that Jean was the one I would ask to my fourteenth-birthday supper, my father's face showed that he dreaded it. I dreaded it, too, a little bit.

Duncan, of course, when he heard about it, got a bright idea. His turn of mind that summer was one where everything that came to his attention had to be connected in some way to his magic show. He would ask Jean to be his Floating Lady. He was so excited about the notion that he drove me up to old Mrs. Sharp's house that Saturday so I could ask Jean to the supper and so he could get a fresh look at her to see how she'd work on stage. He didn't get out of the car, but while I was talking to Jean on her grandmother's front porch I could feel Duncan staring at us from the car window. Then, driving up to the schoolhouse, Duncan chattered away about Jean, how it was great she was so thin and wouldn't be likely to break down the Floating Lady apparatus, as we'd both joked that Toots might have done, and how Jean's "ethereal face," as he put it, would appeal to the audience. He'd stopped thinking about a Rosemary audience, which would be made up mostly of a bunch of antsy, loud-mouthed, bad-smelling, runny-nosed kids, Jeep Alley, Big-Face Limeberry, Thelma Darby and all her freckle-faced family, Mr. and Mrs. Pug Jones and Buntsy, people like that. Duncan was thinking about *audience* in the way they probably thought about it in Charlottesville.

He had this hyperbolic way of talking about everybody: Will Greenwood was the greatest drum major in the history of his high school, Bobby Langston was a fearless and diabolical genius, and so on. About Jean Sharp, I heard him telling our mother in the kitchen, "She's truly beautiful, don't you think?" This was on my birthday, just before Jean's grandmother drove her up to our house, and my father and I, in the living room, exchanged glances when we heard Duncan talking like that. We knew Jean wasn't "truly beautiful." She was just a girl who was visiting in our town. Duncan didn't have to exaggerate what she was just because he wanted her to be in his show. But my father and I were used to his ways that summer. We were grateful to him for doing most of the talking when Jean first walked into our house.

She had on another sundress, this one white with a sort of primly high front to it. It set off her tanned shoulders and face, her dark hair. Something about the way that dress fit her at the arms bothered me, though. It made a loose place where, I knew, if I looked at the right angle, I'd see her breast, or what should have been her breast.

There were girls in my classes at school whose breasts or bras I'd strained my neck trying to get a peek at, but they weren't like Jean. I didn't want to see into her dress, but sitting beside her at the table, I could hardly help noticing that opening every time I cast my eyes in her direction. To make things worse, I became aware of the sounds my father was making as he ate.

Courtly man though he was, his table manners, or rather the things that went on between him and the food on his plate, were pretty crude. He took large bites of things, and there was a kind of liquid inhaling noise that went with each bite. Often he chewed with his mouth open, so that you could hear it, and he liked to roll the food around in his mouth so that he made sloshing noises. It bothered me even though I knew why he did it. It was the result of his courtliness: his way of signaling to my mother that he liked the food was to make eating noises that expressed his pleasure, his gratitude to her for cooking the food for him. The noises had to be loud enough for her to hear him at the opposite end of the table, and I expect they were that evening, even though I knew he was holding back on Jean's account.

I was thinking about asking to be excused when suddenly Duncan asked Jean if she would be his Floating Lady, and she choked on a sip of iced tea.

She was all right, of course. Nobody ever died of iced tea going down the wrong way, at least not that I know of, and you would think the incident—Jean gasping and coughing into her napkin, my father and brother and I rising and coming around behind her chair, ready to pound on her back (though not one of us was going to touch those elegant shoulders unless she got really serious about her choking), my mother coming around the table, too, carrying her napkin for some reason and saying, "Oh, you poor dear, you poor thing"—you'd think the incident would have humanized us all. It didn't. There was a short moment after Jean recovered and we'd all gone back to our places when nobody made a sound, one of those embarrassing lulls in the conversation that are usually broken by somebody's polite giggle. In this case my mother managed a feeble "Well . . . ," and then we had more silence before we fell back to eating, and my father's mouth noises recommenced.

After a while Jean managed to squeak out to Duncan that, yes, she would be happy to be his Floating Lady, and he was released from responsibility for her condition. He went on with his inflated jabbering about the show. But because she had made such a red-faced, watery-eyed, spluttering spectacle of herself, she who was as serene as a piece of sculpture in every other circumstance of my seeing her, Jean now was repulsive to me. Sitting beside her, I lost my appetite.

My mother must also have experienced some kind of pivotal moment that summer evening when Jean Sharp choked in our dining room. That was the last angel food cake with pink icing she ever made for my birthday, though I have never stopped thinking of it as the only legitimate kind of birthday cake.

Next morning, as usual, Duncan and I walked down to the post office where I waited with him while he waited for his ride to Pendleton's quarry. It was an occasion for talking about the magic show. He'd glance at his letter from Susan, if he got one. Then, when he left, I'd take my parents' mail back up the hill to our house.

That morning, though, Duncan had to sign for a little package from Susan. He opened it while he and I were discussing what we were going to do about the kids who'd go around behind the schoolhouse to try to peek in the windows and cracks in the doors to see how the tricks worked. All of a sudden he was holding the diamond ring in his fingers, and I was looking at it, and it was registering on both of us what that meant.

"Aw God, Duncan," I said, "that's a shame." I didn't know what else to say. I wanted to put my arm around his shoulder, but we weren't that kind of a family, and this was in the post office anyway. So I just got out of there as quick as I could and left him standing there staring at the ring with no expression on his face.

I guess he went to work, though I don't know how he got through the day. He came home at the regular time, and he sat with us at the table in the kitchen where we ate supper. But he just dangled his fork over his food and wouldn't eat, wouldn't talk. We'd gotten used to all his jabber-jabber, as my father called it, and the three of us had a hard time filling up the silence. We'd have understood if he'd called off the show. We'd have even understood if he'd taken the car out, gotten drunk, and run it up the side of a tree—there was a tradition of that kind of behavior in our county.

But Duncan was his own man. He worked harder than ever on the magic show, and he said what was necessary to make me work harder on it, too. We'd begun rehearsing in earnest. It wasn't fun for us anymore, what with him losing his temper and going off to sulk when one of us made a mistake. "There is no margin for error in magic," he spat at me once when I lost my balance on the tiny little platform of the Chinese Disappearing Cabinet and put a foot down where the whole audience would have seen it.

Toots asked him to leave the auditorium while she ran through her tap numbers. She said they weren't magic, and she didn't want to know what he thought if she made a mistake. I was surprised when he agreed to leave, and I found that my pleasure in watching the little shimmering of her thighs increased with Duncan out of the room. When I went outside to tell him Toots was finished, I saw him walking over at the far end of the red-dirt elementary-school playground. He had his head down, and I first thought maybe he was crying and then that maybe he was thinking real hard about something. But then I could see little puffs of red dust coming up from his footsteps, and I knew he was stomping the ground, was raging to himself. I went back inside and waited for him to come back in on his own.

I had become a good deal more objective about Jean Sharp by that time. I didn't like to be around her, but I continued to think that I ought to be attracted to her. She was prettier in the face than Toots Polk, and I knew I ought to like looking at her just as much as I liked looking at Toots. But I didn't. The *didn't* and the *ought to* canceled each other out, and I felt nothing.

One night Herky Thompson and Toots took Jean and me out with them on a double date to the drive-in. (Toots's mother made them do it, I expect, because she didn't trust Herky, who was from Piney.) After dark, Jean and I sat in the back seat doing our best to concentrate on *Miss Tatlock's Millions* while Herky and Toots coiled around each other in Toots's corner of the front seat.

I snuck my arm around Jean—she was wearing a sweater —and though I knew she was aware of my arm, I felt no loosening of her good posture, no impulse on her part to lean my way. At the time I resented her for that coldness, but later I decided that she was in the right: she felt no real affection or desire in that arm behind her, those fingers lightly touching her shoulder. She didn't respond because I didn't offer her any part of myself to which she could respond.

All through the final rehearsals Duncan growled at us and cursed under his breath and once put his fist through one of the flats so that we had to repair it. Jean and Toots and I had grown frightened of him. Jean, who rarely said much, told Toots and me that she thought he was going to scare the audience right out of their seats. Toots nodded. I thought about telling them how it had been, earlier in the summer, when Duncan and I had performed "Unchained Melody" to the empty auditorium, but I didn't.

I opened the show out in front of the curtain, ignoring the giggles that Thelma Darby started in the audience when I stepped into the spotlight. I couldn't see past the first row anyway, though my father had passed back the word that we had a full house. I lifted my trumpet and silenced everybody with "It's Cherry Pink and Apple Blossom White."

I finished, the curtain opened, and there was "Duncan the Great" standing in his tuxedo at center stage with Toots a step or two to the side holding the top hat out of which shortly Duncan would yank the three-pound white rabbit I'd bought from Gilmer Hyatt two weeks ago. But he had time for small talk, or "patter," as magicians call it, before the trick. In the most lighthearted tone I'd ever heard him use, he paid me a compliment: "That's Reed Bryant, my brother, ladies and gentlemen, and isn't he some musician?" I got another feeble little round of applause, along with a couple of jeers that I ignored.

Jean really didn't have many duties for the show. She assisted Duncan for a couple of little tricks, but she didn't have any talents that we really needed; so she spent a lot of time standing around near me when I was offstage. Sometimes it was pitch dark back there when Duncan was doing one of the tricks with flames or working with a deck of cards in the spotlight out front. I could feel Jean standing there with me and reminding me of how much I dreaded the Floating Lady trick.

Toots and I were both assistants for that one. We were to pull the chairs out from each end of the Floating Lady's little platform. Toots was at Jean's head, and I was at her feet. I'd bargained with Toots to trade sides, but Duncan hadn't allowed it. I had to get back to the lighting board immediately after the trick to douse the lights, and so it had to be the feet side for me. I had been anxious all through the rehearsals when Jean had worn shorts or slacks, because I knew that in the performance she was to wear a dress. There was a good chance I'd have to see all the way to the north pole, whether

I wanted to or not, and in front of half the town of Rosemary. In any circumstance Jean was a girl up whose dress I did not want to see.

The apparatus for the Floating Lady was heavy and elaborate, because of course it had to hold the lady up, but it had to be so cleverly arranged and concealed that the audience couldn't see it or imagine how it might be set up. Duncan had to brace himself against part of it and stand so that he hid one huge black pipe from the audience. Even then there had to be a four-by-four post holding that thing down behind the rear curtain and braced against the top of a window well. In rehearsal, Toots and I had laughed because all those pipes looked so crude to us that we couldn't believe anybody would ever be fooled. Duncan assured us that the trick would work.

In the performance Duncan and Toots and I were sweating out there under the lights. When Jean in her yellow sundress walked out on stage, she was loudly and somewhat lewdly cheered, but then something about her appearance quieted the audience right down. She really did appear to fall under Duncan's hypnotic spell when he had her sit and then lie down on the platform. Toots fixed Jean's dark hair to lie prettily at the side of her head, and Jean's face and body became waxen, spiritless.

A hush came down over the audience when Toots removed the first chair. Duncan, standing directly behind her, kept his hands held high over Jean while she lay there, and he looked like a crazy preacher held in a spell himself. I looked up at his face then, just before I was to pull my chair. Duncan was charged with some kind of emotion I'd never seen in anybody. I knew that part of it must have had to do with Susan O'Meara, but another part of it was willing that illusion into being: Jean Sharp was by God going to float in the air on the stage of Rosemary Elementary School!

With exaggerated wariness, I removed my chair. Jean wobbled a little bit. Then she held steady. A noise came from the audience, as if everyone had inhaled at once. Clarence Shinault, who'd gone through seventh grade with Duncan, said clearly from way in the back, "Gah-odd *damn*, Duncan."

Gravely, Duncan passed the hoop, with agonizing slowness, from Jean's feet to her head and then back again from her head to her feet. Then he held the hoop up for everyone to see. The applause came just when it should have, Toots and I put our chairs back under the platform, Jean awoke from her spell, smiled, and began climbing down while I skipped back to the lighting board. The trick was over, and I couldn't remember whether or not I'd seen up Jean's dress.

In the week or two before he went back to Charlottesville, thanks to his success with the show, Duncan recovered some of his good spirits. Once he even asked me why I wasn't trying to see more of "The Exquisite Miss Sharp," as he had taken to calling her. I wouldn't have been inclined to explain it to him even if I had understood my feelings about her and even if he had been free enough of his own troubles to be more than halfway interested.

It was my father who gave me the most comfort in that time. Even earlier in the summer he'd started helping me, at the end of the terrible birthday supper when my mother had herded us all into the living room to chat with Jean before she went home. We sat there for an excruciating length of time. I found myself copying my father's manner. I agreed with things Duncan said, things my mother said, and especially with any slight remark of Jean's. Once, the rhythm of conversation demanded that I say something, and so I asked Jean a question about Palm Beach, then pretended to listen while she, with much graceful gesturing of her slender arms and hands, tried to make us understand where in the city she lived and how far that was from the actual beach.

When my father stood up to signal that he wished the occasion to be over, I was the first one to rise and second his motion. Duncan wanted to ride with us on the way over to Jean's grandmother's house so that he could tell her more about the magic show. I'd have been glad to have him along, but my mother put a hand on his sleeve, and he said that, well, now he remembered he had a letter he had to write before he went to sleep.

Outside, standing by the car, my father instructed Jean and me to ride in the back seat. By that time the fireflies were out, the bats were swooping over our heads, it was warm, and there was the scent of honeysuckle over the whole yard, but Jean seemed glad to be climbing into the car. When my father saw that she and I weren't going to have much to say to each other on the drive across the ridge and around the town, he turned on the radio. I've always been grateful to him for that, because I know for a fact that he hated the car radio, especially the hillbilly and rhythm & blues stations that were all we could get at night in our part of the country.

In the cool air I walked Jean up onto her grandmother's front porch, said a quickly retreating goodnight, and scuttled back to sit in the front seat with my father. In his kindness he neither asked me anything nor said a word to me. He'd turned off the radio, and he took his time driving back home. The two of us were quiet, except once when we came to a place where we could see a light way up on the hill at our house.

I said, "I'll bet that's the light in Duncan's room," and my father chuckled and said yes, he guessed Duncan was writing that letter to Charlottesville. That was the night before Duncan got the ring back in the mail from Susan O'Meara, and it was several months before the night he sent Bobby Langston with his squirrel-rifle up on Afton Mountain to wait for him and Susan. It was almost a full year before Duncan flunked out of the University of Virginia. That night, sitting at his bedside table to write that letter to Susan, all Duncan knew that was coming to him was his magic show. My father and I kept driving slowly around the ridge, both he and I watching the road in the headlights and occasionally glancing out our side windows at the dark. Then, at almost exactly the same moment, though our tunes were different, we each began whistling through our teeth.

The

Undesirable

I got over to the side of the road as far as I could, into the grass and the weeds, but my father steered the car over that way, too. Through the windshield I could see his work hat, the shadow of his face and shoulders, the specks of light that were his glasses. I pushed right up against the fence, squeezed into the honeysuckle vines. In a bright haze of sunlight I watched him come at me, the green hood of the Ford growing huge as it came close enough for me to see the waves of heat rising from it. Then he swerved the car over to the middle of the driveway and stopped it beside me. I could see him, in his khaki work clothes, shifting to neutral, pulling the emergency brake, sliding over to the passenger side of the front seat, picking up his dinner-bucket to hold in his lap. He waited for me while I scuffled in the vines and trash beside the fence to reach my glasses.

"You weren't scared, were you?" he asked when I opened the door. There was that sharp smell in the car with him.

Sometimes I imagined, when he came home from work, that there was a coating of gray dust all over him. I got in behind the steering wheel and slammed the door. Every day now I met him at the head of our driveway and drove the car the quarter of a mile in to our house. I was practice-driving with him.

"I knew you wouldn't hit me," I said. When I said it, I knew it was true, sitting there beside him with the sunlight coming down through the trees onto the gravel road in front of us. My father scooted down to rest his head against the back of the seat. He took off his glasses and rubbed the two spots they had dented into the bridge of his nose. He wasn't going to hit me with the car. He'd never even hit me with his hand except once, when I was eight and I'd splashed bathwater on him. I said it again, "I knew you wouldn't hit me." I put the car into low and started it moving, concentrating on easing the clutch out. Then the car jerked. I said "Damn car." My father chuckled to himself, his hat down over his eyes.

I was soon going to be fifteen, which was how old you had to be to get a driver's license. My father might have made me wait until I was older. "You're like a stick of dynamite just waiting for somebody to come along and light your fuse. That somebody isn't going to be me," he said. I thought he understood a little of what it was like to live in Rosemary but go to high school in Madison, twenty miles away. Sometimes, when I was especially restless and jittering my foot or twirling my glasses around in my hand, I would see him looking at me.

Though he was what my grandfather called a fair-sized man, six feet tall and 190 pounds, my father had delicate features. In our hallway was a picture of him and my mother when they were first married, when my mother was fifteen and my father was twenty-one; my mother looked beautiful and much older than fifteen, but my father was even more boyish-looking than I was, I thought. He had a quick temper. He'd raise his voice to yell at Duncan or me. I had heard him yell into the phone at some man who had called him up from the carbide plant at suppertime. "Hell's bells!" my father would say; Duncan and I thought that was hilarious, always giggled when he said it. The skin of my father's body was pale; he wore a hat to keep the sun off his face and kept his shirtsleeves rolled down even on the hottest days. Whenever I saw the muscles of his arms or his legs, they looked to me stringy and slight. But when I'd been smaller, he had sometimes taken my shoulder or my elbow or my knee and squeezed, saying that he was testing my bones. Then his hands had felt powerful to me. I'd tried to imagine my father fistfighting with some of the workmen at the carbide plant, but I couldn't really see it.

I never had reason to fear my father. But my brother and I did speculate about him. One morning a couple of years ago, Duncan had told me a story while we were standing down on the highway waiting for the school bus. It wasn't a story so much as it was a fact. In the full-length mirror of my grandmother's wardrobe were two bullet holes. They had been put there by my father, who'd used the .22 pistol my grandfather kept in the drawer of his bedside table. Duncan had worried that information out of my grandmother, and I admired him for it. I had seen the holes myself, I had had some curiosity about them, but I had never thought to ask anyone about them. Duncan said, "Now what do you suppose could have made him shoot into a mirror that way?" I didn't know. I didn't dare even venture a guess.

Driving the car home wasn't difficult after I got it started rolling. I could put it into second and high gears easily because the way was downhill, along the ridge of our hill where we could look down and see most of the houses in Rosemary in the valley below us. It looked like pictures I'd seen of villages where they made wine in Europe, except their hillsides were lined with vineyards and ours were mostly fields of broomsage and scrub cedars, cow pastures, cornfields, trash piles, gatherings of junked cars, and back behind us the smoke of the carbide plant rising up from the two tall stacks.

When we got home, the hardest thing of all was getting into the garage. That involved making the turn just exactly right, judging the straightening precisely, getting the rear wheels up over the hump without killing the engine, and then getting the car stopped before it plowed through the far wall. My father had started letting me do it. Today he didn't even watch me; he kept his head resting on the seat, his hat over his eyes. Then, when I turned off the ignition, he asked me, "Did you get it in all right, Son?"

He'd started using that tone of voice with me when he taught me to play his alto saxophone. When I'd just turned thirteen, he said I needed something to occupy my mind. We walked over to my grandfather's house, to the parlor, where he lifted the black leather carrying case out from behind the piano. He let me open it and hold it in my lap while he told me about it. The case was lined with dark purple velvet, and the horn, in two pieces, lay in exactly fitted compartments. There was a smell in there of age, of something valuable. The saxophone was still shiny, undented, a burnished silver with fancy engraving and a gold-plated inside of the bell. My father had sent it to the factory in Elkhart, Indiana, and had it put in perfect condition before he had packed it away. He taught me how to assemble the neck and the mouthpiece, to wet the reed and fasten it on. He showed me how the fingering worked to close the pads or open them. Then he put it in his mouth and played "Little Brown Jug." He handed it to me, and I made it squawk.

But in a month I could play "Little Brown Jug," "The Darktown Strutters' Ball," "The St. Louis Blues," and "Lullabye and Goodnight." My father had stacks of old sheet music and a box of arrangements he'd made for his own band. He said I was the fastest learner he'd ever encountered. He arranged an appointment with the Madison High School Band Director, Mr. Oliver, and took me to Madison to audition. While Mrs. Oliver fried chicken in the kitchen, my father and Mr. Oliver sat on the living-room sofa and listened to me play through "I Dream of Jeannie with the Light Brown Hair."

My father had packed that saxophone away at his parents' house when he began working at the carbide plant, just after he married my mother. He'd begun work there as a construction foreman. He became Personnel Manager, then Assistant Engineer, then Plant Engineer, and finally, a few years ago, Works Manager, supervisor of the whole thing. Most of the people in Rosemary had felt it was inevitable that my father would become the boss of the carbide plant, but he didn't like for anybody to say anything that suggested he hadn't earned every one of his promotions. All my life he'd smelled of carbide, a sharp, nose-pinching odor that wasn't unpleasant after you got used to it. I could remember, from when I was a little boy being carried in his arms, the smooth starched surface of his khaki workshirts, the roughness of his bearded cheek, the smell of his sweat, cigarettes, carbide. Once he brought home a small can of carbide, the kind miners use in their headlamps, he said. He took Duncan and me out on the back porch, poured some of the gray, crumbly stuff out of the can into a bucket of water. The lumps of carbide fizzed and bubbled like dry ice, made a kind of steam. Then he struck a match, and there was a flame over the water. "It stinks," Duncan said. We were both impressed by my father's demonstration. We asked him to do it for us again the next day when he came home from work, and he did, but he wouldn't anymore after that.

He complained, getting out of the car, that he didn't have enough room between the door and the side of the garage, but I noticed that he was managing it anyway. I knew he was trying to josh me into a good mood. We went in then. My mother was in the kitchen, fixing supper. She had flour on her hands and held them away from my father while they kissed. While he was washing his hands and rinsing out his thermos bottle, he told her what he'd done, scaring me by driving the car at me. He said he wanted to see how I handled myself in an emergency. I knew he was telling her about it because he was uncomfortable with it. He wanted to see if telling my mother about it would bring back the joke he'd intended. I wanted to tell him not to worry. When he stood in the kitchen like that, after work, talking with my mother, as if by talking he could change himself from how he had to be at work to how he had to be at home, I was always pleased with him. But I didn't say anything. And by my mother's silence, I knew she didn't approve of his joke. She would tell him what she thought when I wasn't around.

While he was talking, she cleaned her own hands off, got him a beer and a glass and handed them to him. He made his usual offer to help her in the kitchen. She made her usual refusal, telling him to go on and get out of her way. I followed him into his study where he went to sit at his desk and read the paper. For several years my father had complained that his living-room chair wasn't comfortable. One Christmas my mother had gotten him a new easy chair, but, even though he hadn't complained, he'd squirmed and fidgeted in it. Finally he'd taken to sitting at his desk in the study to relax after work. He turned on the desk light and spread out the paper. I took a seat behind him and waited for him to offer me some of his beer. I breathed on my glasses, loudly, and wiped them with my handkerchief. Finally he did make the offer, and I took a gulp. I stood beside him with my hand on his shoulder while he read. I wanted him to know I didn't hold it against him, the joke with the car. I wanted to stay on his good side until I had my driver's license. He asked me what I'd done that day, and I started telling him about mowing old Mrs. Oakes's yard. While I was talking to him, he took out his pen and started working the crossword puzzle. I stopped halfway through a sentence and waited to see what would happen.

"Dad?" I said.

He grunted.

"Dad, are you listening?" I asked him.

"What?" he said, still in that preoccupied tone of voice.

"Why'd you ask me if you didn't want to hear?" I shouted at him. I went upstairs to my room, stomped on the steps and shut the door hard. I knew my mother would probably hold it against him that he'd provoked me. Upstairs I got out the saxophone and started practicing scales on the high notes. Then I worked on the saxophone breaks to "Burn That Candle" and "Blue Monday," two of my father's least favorite songs. Then Mother called me down for supper, and I came to the table. My father, with his face somewhat drawn, said grace.

Dinner was spaghetti with my mother's homemade bread. I ate rudely, slurping my noodles into my mouth and splashing sauce until my mother got enough of me and told me to behave at the table. My father chopped his spaghetti into small bites and told us about hiring a new secretary. Mrs. Millgram, the blue-haired lady who my mother said had lovely posture and who had worked at the carbide plant since before my father had come there, had finally retired. He had to find a replacement for her. The other secretary at the carbide plant, dumpy-looking, sour-tempered Mrs. Sharitz, would be there another twenty years before she retired. Of her my father had said, "I don't believe that if Mrs. Sharitz had all day to work on it, she could manage to stick her finger in her eye." Before he went off to the university, Duncan and I had laughed for a couple of days over that, and I still chuckled whenever I saw her. The new secretary my father said he had decided to hire was named Darcy Webster. He looked at my mother and me to see if we knew her.

He said that Darcy Webster was the daughter of Preacher Webster, the Mercy Circuit Methodist minister. That was why we couldn't have known her, because she was from Mercy County, had gone to high school over in Gantley. After that she'd taken a one-year course at Roanoke Business College, then had come home to look for a job. Of the five applicants my father interviewed for the job, Darcy had been by far the best. She typed seventy words per minute, made no errors. She took shorthand. She knew grammar and spelling. She was pleasant, cheerful, and pretty.

"What are you worried about?" my mother asked him.

My father smiled across the table at her. He hadn't said he was worried, but both of us had known that he was.

"That last," he said. "That she's pretty."

Mother raised her eyebrows at him, asking him four or five questions all at once without saying a word aloud.

"There are two hundred and eighty-five men who work at that plant," my father said. "To my certain knowledge, there have been, in the whole time that the plant has been in operation, only three women who have worked there. There's never been a young one. There's never been one who wasn't married. There's never been a pretty one." He took off his glasses, rubbed his eyes and the bridge of his nose, and looked mournfully at the shards of spaghetti on his plate.

"I'll look forward to seeing her," said my mother.

The first time my mother did see Darcy, I was with her. She'd needed the car for shopping, and so she'd taken my father to work that morning. At quitting time, I went with her to meet him. From our house, or from anywhere within ten miles of Rosemary, the smoke from the carbide plant was visible, a thick column of billowing white stuff. On a clear, sunny day, it looked beautiful, like the beginning of a cloud, white the way clouds are sometimes white in the sunlight. If the sky was overcast or if it was raining, then the smoke was gray, ugly stuff, a kind of soupy fog. But this was a clear day in June. My mother and I were both in a jolly mood, turning off the highway onto the carbide road, pulling slowly along past the lines of railroad cars, past the warehouses, over the siding of railroad tracks that went inside the plant fence, past the office buildings and then to the gatehouse where we turned around and parked so as to be able to see my father when he came out. I wanted her to stop the car between the buildings so that I could watch the men working the furnace, walking back and forth around the huge area of electrical fire. She wouldn't do it. Even that far away, sitting in the car, you could feel the heat of the furnace when they were tapping, when there was a great tub of molten stuff suspended in the air above the furnace that the men tipped and poured into containers that were hauled away by other men. My mother hated the heat, said she'd been seeing carbide furnaces long enough to suit her and didn't need to see any more. I liked to watch the men who shoved limestone and coke from up above, who my father said had to take salt tablets every couple of hours and had to wear sheepskin-lined jackets and winter underwear even in summer to hold in the sweat, to be able to stand the heat. I got out and stood behind the car to watch for a while. But then the tapping stopped. The men were about to change shifts. The shrill whistle blew for four-thirty quitting time.

The eight-to-four-thirty shift came out of the gatehouse, men in crumpled and sweated-through work hats, blue jeans or baggy-seated overalls, dark-blue or khaki or gray workshirts, and heavy steel-toed shoes or boots. Many of them nodded to my mother, touched their fingers to their hat brims: Tommy Alley who straightened his shoulders and smiled, Old Man Buck Weatherman whose chin was tucked down into his neck, and Bert Lawson who strutted, even after he'd put in a full day's work. The men came out of the gatehouse in twos and threes and fours, some of them not speaking a word, some joking and laughing, hitching up their pants, clapping each other on the back, dangling their dinner-buckets at the ends of their fingers. Then, in a fresh pink dress with a full skirt, in high-heeled shoes, with her chin up and her shoulders squared, with a ponytail of hair the color of wheat, came Darcy Webster. I'd never seen her before.

There were girls that pretty in my high school, but they were older than me, they didn't know who I was, and I never thought of speaking to them. Darcy gave me a smile and said "Hi!" I tried fixing my face in what I thought was approximately a smile.

She walked to the car window where my mother sat, leaned down, holding her white purse in both hands in front of her, and said, "Hi, are you Mrs. Bryant? I thought so. I'm Darcy Webster." I couldn't hear what my mother said just then. I stood with my hand on the car door for a moment before I got into the back seat. When I did get in and get the door shut, Darcy and my mother were saying their goodbyes. Then Darcy was walking down the road away from us. Men were walking along that way, too; they made way for her, a few of them smiling, speaking, reaching up to touch their hat brims to her. Then she came to her own car and got in it. My mother and I watched her with an attention that demanded silence. We were quiet. My father came to the door on the passenger side and climbed into the front seat.

"What do you think of my poster?" my father asked us while my mother got the car going, driving slowly through the crowd of men, stopping to let cars pull out ahead of her. My father had begun a safety campaign at the carbide plant a couple of years before. The most recent step he'd taken was to install a billboard-sized frame on the side of the main furnace building. The new poster showed a cartoon man, his mouth open as if to shout, his arms gesturing frantically, being pulled into the gears of an evil-looking machine while other cartoon men kept their backs turned to him. The motto of the poster was SAFETY IS EVERYBODY'S BUSINESS.

"That's real nice, Dad," I said. I was just learning the pleasures of sarcasm and ambiguity. He turned around to look at me, but I hid the grin sneaking onto my mouth by pushing my glasses up farther onto my nose.

"If I were you, I'd save my smartness for school," he said, but he wasn't really angry. As long as we were in *If-I-were-you* territory, I was safe.

"We met Darcy," my mother said when she'd gotten the car out of the carbide area, onto the highway. I appreciated her getting the conversation steered that way. I was hungry to hear them talk about Darcy. I was even eager to put in my own opinions. I'd decided that what I thought was prettiest about her was how her light-brown skin looked with that pink dress. I wondered if I would say that aloud. From the tone of my mother's voice, I thought she thought well of Darcy, at least so far. When we talked, in our family, about pretty women, my mother was the final judge, the authority none of us questioned.

"Oh, you did?" My father let the silence hang in the air. I could tell he wanted to know what my mother thought as much as I did.

"A lot of women couldn't get by with wearing that dress," my mother said.

"Let's see now, what . . ."

"The pink one," I said. It was possible that Darcy's dress had gone unnoticed by my father; on the other hand, it was more likely that he was acting as if he'd not paid any attention to it. At any rate, I wanted the conversation to move on.

"Yes, the sleeveless pink dress," my mother said. "She looks striking in it."

"Bad color, huh?" my father asked.

"No, not bad at all. Exactly right, as a matter of fact."

"Too sexy?" he asked. I was glad he brought it up like that. I wanted to see what my mother would say. She was the family authority on matters of sexiness, too.

"No, certainly not," she said. "She could wear that dress to go hear her father preach."

"Well, what?" my father asked.

"Well, nothing," she said. "I said that a lot of women couldn't get by with wearing that dress. I didn't say there was anything wrong with it."

"No, I guess you didn't."

"She handles herself with a great deal of poise, too," my mother said. "She came right up to the car and introduced herself. I'd be happy if I thought any child of mine"—I got a flick of her eyes from the rear-view mirror—"would have manners enough to know how to do that." Manners and poise were high on my mother's list of virtues, especially since Duncan and I didn't have much of either. She seemed to be taking inventory of Darcy's good points, as if she were determined to cover every one of them.

"Good for her," my father said.

"She spoke to me too," I piped up, leaning forward over the front seat between them. That put an end to our discussion of Darcy. I could tell they were saving what else they had to say for some time when I wasn't around to hear them. I was tired of being treated like someone who just wasn't mature enough to hear really important matters of conversation. I wanted to say more, to say something brilliant and stunning, but I wasn't about to let myself blurt out a stupid remark for them to hold against me.

My birthday was a hot July day. That morning my father drove me to the Madison courthouse to take the test for my driver's license. The windshields of the cars we passed glared so brightly that I had to squint my eyes. When we stopped in the courthouse parking lot, the pavement was soft and gummy under our feet. It felt good to go inside the cool stone and the vaulted ceiling of the courthouse. I knew I would pass the written part of the test; in school I enjoyed taking tests more than listening to the teachers. This one was easy. I got them all correct except for one, and the testing lady bragged on me for my high score. A large blond state trooper walked back outside with me. We both nodded at my father, sitting out there on the steps, fanning himself with his hat. Neither the policeman nor I spoke out loud to him; he might have been somebody we knew or didn't know. But I could see him giving me his solemn look meant to inspire confidence. I kept wondering what that state trooper, with his perfect uniform and his kind, official voice, was thinking about me. I put the car in gear, all right. I drove it around the block, stopping for lights, giving the correct hand-signals. Then I drove back to the parking lot where a yellow rectangle was painted on the concrete, and I parallel-parked. The trooper climbed out, saying over his shoulder, "Come on in, Son, and we'll write out your license." I was grinning like a fool when we passed my father that second time.

My father and I went home, with me driving the highway from Madison to Rosemary for the first time. When we got to our house, Mother sent me back in the car by myself to drive down to Elkins's store to buy eggs, cream, sugar, and rock salt for an ice-cream celebration. Down there, trying to park, I hit the back of Mrs. Peacock's old battered Plymouth; it made a loud bang, both cars rocked up and down, and people trotted outside the store to have a look. There were dents in both cars, but Mrs. Peacock folded her arms over the top of her bosom and said, "Lord, Reed, don't worry about it, Honey. One more dent in my car won't hurt a thing." I was grateful to her and felt a little guilty about always having thought of her as a fat, pig-eyed old woman. I didn't report that incident to my father, but the next day, first thing when I saw him before suppertime, he caught my eye and said, "Dent in the right front fender."

"Yes sir," I said. "That's mine."

"Yours?"

"Yes sir. I mean, I put it there."

He shook his head at me and didn't ask any more questions.

Back before I was born, Rosemary had been an iron-smelting town. In the other direction from the carbide plant were acres and acres of ripped-up, rocky land that had been surface-mined for low-grade iron ore. Almost all of the town had once been owned by the Pittsburgh Industrial Metals Corporation, which went out of business before it finished what it had in mind for Rosemary. On our side of the carbide plant, the Pittsburgh company had built large houses for its managers and engineers; we lived in one of those houses, my grandparents in another. The company had made plans for where other different sorts of people were going to live. Pittsburgh Industrial Metals had planned for Rosemary to grow. Streets were laid out, named, constructed, and paved, but no houses were ever built on them. There was a stone foundation of a huge building on a large plot of land near our house; my grandfather said that was to have become the Rosemary Hotel. He laughed when he told about it. Now there were simply small roads with square corners to them, roads that had been given names years before by someone in Pittsburgh. Most of the names were never used; some of them were never even known by the people in Rosemary. Many of those roads had turned back to dirt roads and then turned further back to grass paths that were used only occasionally by people walking, say, from a house in Rakestown or in Slabtown down to the river to fish, or by a child wandering or wanting to take a shortcut from where he was to somewhere else.

I enjoyed driving those roads, downhill toward the river bottom and the flat valley-land along which the railroad tracks ran. The carbide plant was built in this place so as to have access to railroad shipping, to use the river water to cool its furnaces, to use the river's electrical power from its dams upstream, to empty its sewage into the river. I had been driven back and forth to and from the carbide plant in cars with my parents, and sometimes my grandparents, for as long as I could remember. To be driving by myself, even if only the distance of a mile and a half between our house and the plant and even if in my father's car, I took as a sign that I was soon going to have my own life.

On the small road in to the carbide plant, speed limits were posted at fifteen miles per hour, another part of my father's safety campaign. I was careful to observe that restriction. I was always hungry to see everything around that place anyway. Driving slowly made it easier to look. Men I passed would raise a hand to me, or to my father's car. Their way of waving was different for me by myself than it would have been if my father had been riding with me. Either way, the gestures the men made were ones that I admired, a hand signaling an exact measure of respect and courtesy, of pride and humility. I was not able to duplicate their gestures or to make one of my own that would do. My waves seemed to me always a little too eager, too attentive. If I passed a group of men and waved to them, I imagined that my wave provoked them to talk about me when I had gone by. If I heard laughter from them, I became aware of my glasses; my neck and ears burned. I could make up the things they might say: "Not going to be the man his father is." "That's right. Little bookworm. Little horn-player." "His grandfather don't even know him, can't recognize him." They had their opinions of me, I knew they did, those men who worked for my father, with their rolling walks, their hats pushed forward on their foreheads, their sleeves rolled up over tattooed, veined, muscled arms.

I turned the car around beside the gatehouse, parked it with its nose pointing back toward home, turned off the engine but left the ignition key turned on. I had to hear one of my necessary radio programs, the request hour on the Madison station. Lots of kids who called in requests were my high-school classmates, Madison kids mostly, but now and then somebody from Rosemary would get his name on the air. I was thinking about school, about how it would be to be able to drive a car there sometimes, because when the term started, I would be a sophomore. I kept the radio turned down to what my father would have called a reasonable level; he was very big on being reasonable and moderate, on exercising good judgment, in his discussions with me. I slumped down in the seat, looked out away from the plant and down into the field between the railroad tracks and the river. The water was running low and muddy, the way it always did during dog days. On the other side, the mountain rose almost straight out of the water, part of it upriver from the plant being sheer cliff-face of brown and gray rock. Out over the mountain the rolling column of carbide smoke rose, thick and solid-looking as spun glass, going out and up as far as I could see. I felt someone touch my arm at the window and turned around to see Darcy standing there close enough to bite me if she'd been a snake.

"Reed?" she said. She wore a pleated white blouse and a skirt with small colored flowers on it. She had an earnest expression on her face. She didn't seem quite as poised as she had when she'd introduced herself to my mother that day. I nodded vigorously and reached to turn the radio off. I tried to think of something to say to her that she would like, something that would make her want to stay there. Because of her hair's being pulled back, I'd always thought of her eyes as small and slanted like an oriental woman's, but up close they were large and brown with flecks of green in them. "I don't know why I listen to that stuff," I said. I pushed my glasses up onto my nose and wished immediately that I hadn't done it, could see my toothy expression from her point of view.

"You're Reed, aren't you?"

"Yes, ma'am," I said. I didn't know why she was so concerned about what my name was. "The same name as my grandfather. It's his name, too. But nobody calls him that."

She smiled then, to herself, as if I'd said something that only she knew was funny. She crossed her arms in front of her, drew the white pleated blouse down tight over her chest, and asked, "How old are you, Reed?"

"Fifteen," I said. "I got my license last month."

"I'm nineteen," she said. "Just four years older."

"Huh," I said. I hadn't thought of her as being just nineteen. I'd thought of her as being a woman. It made me feel better to know she was just four years older, but I still couldn't think of anything to say that I thought would make her be interested in me.

"Your father's told me about you," she said, a tease coming into her voice.

"What did he say?" I asked. I really did wonder what my father told other people about me.

"Well, let me see," She put her finger on her chin. She was trying to act like she knew a lot, but I figured out then that my father hadn't really told her much about me, probably just my name.

"He said you played in the band." Darcy said that too eagerly, as if she were proud of herself for having remembered it.

"Yes, that's right," I said. "I play alto saxophone." Coming out of the gatehouse was my father. I couldn't help but let my eyes go past Darcy's shoulder to look at him, to see what he would think of her standing there talking with me. But he was listening to Mr. Atkins and Tommy Alley. I couldn't tell if he'd even noticed me. Darcy saw where I was looking, turned and looked too, then touched my elbow with her hand and said, "There's your father." When I caught her eye, we both realized what a dumb thing that was to say to me, and so we both laughed about it. "Time to go home," she said. "Goodbye, Reed." She pronounced my name very positively.

"See you, Darcy," I called out, as my father climbed into the car beside me. I wanted him at least to notice that I called his secretary by her first name.

"See you tomorrow, Mr. Bryant," Darcy called to my father, waving to him and walking ahead of us toward her own car. My father lifted a hand and gave her a smile, one that I knew he had to force himself to hang on his face, but as we pulled out it was easy to see he wasn't thinking much about Darcy.

"Have to change that," he said, looking at the new sign on the warehouse building we were driving past; it said THIS PLANT HAS GONE   DAYS WITHOUT AN ACCIDENT. In the blank space hung a metal plate with the number 109 on it.

"What?" I asked.

"Aw, Cecil Campbell," he said in a tone that if I hadn't known him all my life I would have thought meant anger of the deepest sort. "Got his fingers chopped off in the can shop this afternoon. These two." He lifted his own hand, with the middle and index fingers raised, to show me.

"God," I said. It was what we'd taken to saying at band practice when someone was out of tune or hitting a lot of wrong notes. My father gave me a look that registered for both of us how wrong it sounded in the car at that moment.

"The cutter in the can shop comes down every forty-five seconds to cut the tin. If your fingers are there, then it cuts them, too. Everybody who works there knows that."

"Nothing to be done for Mr. Campbell?" I asked. I swung the car into our driveway, another square corner.

"Nothing I know of," my father said, his voice tired. He settled back in the seat but didn't let his head rest the way he did sometimes. "Cecil Campbell was working in that can shop thirteen years when Tommy Alley's daddy lost his fingers in exactly the same way. You just can't get to daydreaming in the can shop. Cecil knew exactly what it meant when that cutter came down on his hand."

"Yes sir," I said.

"Fool," my father said.

"Sir?"

"They said he shut the machine off, scooped his fingers up with his good left hand, ran outside, and threw them across the railroad tracks there just outside the shop. They said he was cussing like a sailor."

"God," I said.

"But when I saw him in the first-aid room, he was as docile as a kitten. Kept saying, 'I'm sorry, Mr. Bryant, I'm sorry.' " My father put his head back then, took off his glasses, and put his hat down over his eyes, which didn't make sense since we were about to come around the last curve to our house. "I told him, 'Cecil,' I said, 'you don't have to be sorry to me.' "

At the end of August, just before school started, we traded cars. Mother said she was sure my father was doing it to cheer himself up. Two more accidents happened at the plant the week after Cecil Campbell lost his fingers, and union negotiations were coming up in October. Mother didn't object to the trade, though. It was a pleasure to see my father behind the wheel of his bright blue 1957 Dodge Coronet, with its streamlined fins going straight back from the rear window to the taillights, and with push-button drive. My father'd never had a car with any kind of automatic transmission, let alone push-button drive. He leaned back in the seat, straightened his arms at the wheel, and pushed the D button with exaggerated casualness.

The first time I drove it to the plant, Darcy came out of the gatehouse smiling like somebody was going to give that new car to her. She'd heard about it already, I could tell, but she asked me questions about it, talked with me enthusiastically. When my father came out, he did not go around to the passenger side as he usually did. He stepped right up beside

Darcy and asked me to scoot over. When he got in behind the wheel, he stayed there talking to Darcy for a long while, leaning back in the seat with his arms straightened at the wheel. Darcy praised the car some more, then she bent down to speak to me across my father's arms. " 'Bye, Reed," she said. I found myself blushing with my father's eyes on me.

The first week of September I convinced my parents to let me take the car to Madison for a night meeting of the Beta Club. If it hadn't been an honor to be invited to join the Beta Club, I wouldn't have been allowed. In Madison the Rosemary kids had a reputation for being slow and stupid in school, but there were three of us from Rosemary whose averages had been good enough for Beta Club. Fat Bobby Sloan and Patch Whitacre, who had red hair and freckles and played trombone in the band, were going to ride over with me to the meeting. It was a Wednesday evening, just turning twilight as we cruised the highway, all three of us slicked up in our good clothes, ready to be honored for our intelligence.

The meeting, however, in the high-school cafeteria, was a disappointment. None of the Madison kids had dressed up, and Wayne Dillard, the president, called out, when we walked in early, "Hello, hicks." All three of us were used to being kidded about being from the sticks, being farmers, being hicks. But Wayne wouldn't have called out like that if Bobby Sloan hadn't been with us; Bobby really was kind of backwards in his manners. Because Patch and I were in the band, people sometimes even forgot that we lived in Rosemary. The Beta Club meeting lasted just long enough for them to call the roll and to swear in the new members. We were in a good mood from all the giggling and the horsing around and the yelling when the meeting was adjourned. When we walked out of the cafeteria, there was still an edge of red sunlight in the sky west of town. Bobby and Patch and I agreed it was a shame to go home that early, even if it was a school night.

Bobby asked us to take him down to the High Hat to get him something to eat. Patch and I laughed at him, told him he was fat, told him people in Madison would always think he was a hick if the first thing he did when he got to town was go to the High Hat Drive-In and stuff his face with French fries. Bobby was embarrassed and said he hadn't had time to get any supper before he left home. Then Patch and I felt sorry that we'd said those things to him. We all went down to the High Hat and stuffed our faces. We stayed there for a while, kicking around the parking lot, talking to some people we knew, mostly older kids who came down there and hung around for a couple of hours almost every night. Bobby got tired of standing around other people's cars, and so he went to sit in our front seat to wait for Patch and me. Then we prowled around Madison for a while, driving past girls' houses and talking about them. Since Bobby didn't know where anybody lived, Patch and I gave him a town tour, so to speak. We hadn't been in any of those houses, the ones where the more famous of the junior and senior high school girls lived, but we'd had their houses pointed out to us by friends of ours in the band. I was careful on those streets because I'd heard that the Madison cops liked nothing better than catching somebody from Rosemary doing something wrong. When it was almost eleven, and most of the parking places on Main Street were empty, all three of us stopped talking. Bobby said, as if he'd been waiting a long time to bring it up, "Let's go home."

Out on the highway I tried to get back some of the excitement we'd had earlier in the evening. I ran the speed up on that Dodge just to show Patch and Bobby what it would do. Bobby stayed quiet, but Patch lit up a cigarette, switched on the radio, found the Wheeling station, and turned it up loud. Going that fast, it was too cold to keep the windows open, and so Patch and I cranked them closed. The highway was empty and straight out ahead of us. I didn't slow down again, just kept the speedometer on eighty and eighty-five, which was the speed where I could hold it steady. "Bobby, are you scared?" I asked him, and he said no, but I could tell that he was. The road was straight, and the new Dodge didn't show any sign of strain; it felt like it was riding about a foot higher off the ground than it usually did, like it was about to take off and rise up in the beams of light out ahead of us. Patch was saying how the speedometer was funny on those new Dodges anyway, the way there were little boxes that filled up with a bright red color, one box for every five miles of speed.

We came up over a hill. A car was pulling out down there, from a driveway, so slowly it seemed to be almost stopped halfway onto the highway. I could see the red lights, could tell they were barely moving, but it was a long way off. I touched the brake and felt the Dodge pull a little to one side. I put the brake pedal down and held it down, pressing harder and harder on it, seeing the red lights of the car down there get closer a lot faster than I'd thought they would. I felt the wheels go off in gravel, a heavy lurch sideways. Then the car was in a slow, gentle, merry-go-round spin, hitting into the ditch over on Patch's side, then just flopping right up onto its roof, so that all three of us were lying on the car ceiling, with the dash lights and the motor still on, the radio going, the headlights tunneling out at a crazy angle across a field. "Where's your cigarette, Patch?" I asked him. I turned off the radio and the ignition. The silence felt queer.

"I threw it out," he said, his voice calm, still perky, as if he were still having a fine time. Light from somewhere shone on his freckled face, making him look pale and spotted. Gradually I figured out how awkwardly our bodies lay on the car ceiling, how tangled we were with each other.

Then Bobby spoke up, his voice five notes higher than it should have been. "Are you all right? Are you all right?" he shrilled.

"I am," I said, but I didn't know for sure if I was. I couldn't find my glasses, but I hadn't noticed when they'd slipped off. Patch said, "I bumped my knee, but I think I'm O.K." Bobby rasped out loudly, "Thank you, God! Thank you, Jesus!" I tried to get my legs untangled from his. I remembered that Bobby Sloan sometimes went to the Pentecostal Holiness Church, and he was loathsome to me right at that moment.

"My door won't work," I said. Patch rolled his window down and started wriggling out of it. Bobby followed him and took a long time. I waited for him and hated his fatness until he was out of the car. When I got through the window, a man shone a flashlight on me, and another man was standing there watching me on my hands and knees. I still didn't have my glasses and couldn't see anyone clearly; they were shadows until light from the highway caught them. The one with the flashlight asked me if I was the driver. I told him that I was. He said, "Son, you're a damn fool. All three of you boys could have been killed." His voice had an edge of pleasure to it, as if he were saying something about a movie he'd seen and liked.

"Yes sir," I said. I couldn't see him well enough to know if he was the kind of a man I ought to be saying *sir* to or not. And it had not occurred to me until that moment that any of us were in danger. I started to tell the man that it wasn't as bad as he thought it was. But then there was a state policeman to talk to, a small man who came up beside me, spoke quietly, and didn't seem at all angry at me. He crawled into the car to shut off the lights and to be sure the ignition was off. When he started back out of the car, he held out my glasses from the window and called, "Whose are these?" I didn't say anything, just bent and took them from his hand. We all three went to sit in his car, me in front, Bobby and Patch in the back. He looked at each of us carefully, as if he were trying to make some judgment about what kind of boys we were. He asked me to tell him how the accident had happened. He'd parked so that his headlights shone through the dark over onto my father's upside-down car. While I was talking and while Bobby and Patch were talking to him, I had to sit there and look at the wheels and the underside of my father's new Dodge. By the time my father and Bobby's father got there, I had trouble making myself say any words at all. Bobby's father had had to pick up my father and drive him over to where we were. Mr. Sloan was sanctimonious and a leader in the union at the carbide plant. I couldn't look straight at my father.

We boys got out of the car. Bobby went over to talk with his father. Patch came over and stood beside me while my father climbed into the policeman's car to talk with him. Patch and I stood there and watched them through the back window, both of them nodding their heads, my father shaking his every now and then. When he got out, he kept his head turned toward the upside-down car instead of toward me. I decided he was waiting until we were alone. The wrecker came and pulled the car over onto its side and then right side up. The driver of the wrecker said that he was certain the car would be declared a total wreck. "Totaled that thing," Patch said quietly to me.

Bobby's father drove us all home, with only him and Bobby doing the talking, Bobby leaning up from the middle of the back seat to talk to his daddy, my father sitting silent on the passenger side in front. My father insisted that Mr. Sloan let us out at the bottom of our hill, down on the highway. The last thing Mr. Sloan said to us when we got out in the dark was, "We've got a lot to be grateful for tonight, Mr. Bryant."

"Yes, that's right," my father said. "We certainly do, Robert. I thank you for your help." When the car was gone, we stood for a while letting our eyes get used to the dark. We fumbled with the old gate down there, then decided to climb the thing. On the other side we had to stand still a minute to be able to make out the path up the hill to our house, and there my father touched my shoulder. He was awkward about it, and he didn't know what to say. He said, "Reed, Reed," as if he had something else to tell me, but once he'd said my name like that, in that tone of being sorry for both of us, there wasn't anything more for him to say. We went on up the hill in the dark. I told him I was sorry while I was walking behind him, and he said he knew I was, not to worry about it too much. He was out of breath and puffing by the time we reached the porch light my mother had turned on for us.

The judge suspended my driver's license for six months. He fined me fifteen dollars plus costs. He was a young man with short black hair going gray and a ruddy complexion. He said he would have fined me much more than that if I had been an adult, but he understood from talking with the investigating officer that my father would have to pay my fine for me. The judge said he didn't see any use in my father's having to pay a lot of money for my irresponsible behavior. He gave me a stern lecture, told me that the town of Rosemary didn't need any more drivers like me, that it had plenty of them already. He told me he hoped I had learned my lesson. I said I was certain I had. My parents tried to cheer me up, made jokes about how they hadn't liked that old blue car anyway. I told them solemnly that I never wanted to drive again. My mother said she understood how I felt. I doubted that she did, but I kept my mouth shut. We used my grandmother's old black '52 Chrysler for another week, until the new car that my father had ordered to replace the wrecked one came in. The new Dodge was green and white. My father didn't take as much pleasure in it as he had in the old one.

On the school bus, I became known as The Night Rider. The first several days after the wreck were especially humiliating. The bus drove right past my skid-marks on the highway and the wedged-up sod and dirt in the ditch where the car had landed. Rosemary high-school students had to catch one of the two buses that drove to Madison at seven or seven-thirty in the morning. Both buses looped out onto dirt roads to pick up county students from farms or back up in the hills. Kids from Rosemary and from our part of the county had a bad reputation in Madison: they didn't know how to act, didn't know how to dress, misbehaved in class, couldn't learn anything, never knew the answers, used crude language, fought, carried knives, weren't clean. Rosemary kids took a kind of pride in being the outlaws of the consolidated school, dressed like hoods or sluts, told stories about violent and reckless behavior. On my bus Janet Littrel and Judy Statler, who'd gone through grade school with me, clucked their tongues at me, rubbed pointed index fingers, and said, "Shame, shame on you, Reed Bryant." Herbert Blevins, who usually flipped my ears and dared me to do anything in retaliation, or who farted in his hand and then reached up from behind me to put the hand over my nose, asked me to tell him what had happened. I told Herbert that I didn't want to talk about it, but Patch, with whom I usually sat, gave him a full account. Herbert and George Oglesby and Botch Atkins all listened carefully and giggled and clapped me on the shoulder and called me The Night Rider. When Molly Whisnant got on the bus way out in Draper, she looked at me with a big smile on her face and said, "I heard about you, Reed Bryant." I kept my jacket collar turned up, looked out the window, wouldn't talk with anybody, just let Patch do my talking for me. But sitting there on that bus with those Rosemary kids talking about me, I began to feel good, began to feel like an outlaw. In the halls at school, rumors were that I had been traveling at well over a hundred miles an hour when the wreck happened, that I had been drunk, that what had really caused it was that I had been running from the cops.

Bobby Sloan stayed away from me after the wreck; he gave me to understand that he thought I was just fine but that his father had forbidden him to associate with me. But Patch and I became even closer friends. We were both in the band together, we both fancied ourselves pretty good musicians. Sometimes we sneaked out of Phys. Ed. to smoke a cigarette, or we smoked one before band practice or while we were waiting in the windy parking lot to practice the band's marching routines for the football games. Smoking cigarettes made me feel dizzy and powerful. I savored the looks of disapproval I received almost as much as the smoke itself. I imagined myself as having a casual deadliness of appearance with a cigarette in my mouth. I was somebody who'd totaled a car and lived to tell about it.

My mother caught me smoking out behind the garage one Saturday afternoon. She cried, said I was only fifteen, that if I wanted to smoke I had to wait until I was out of her house. I felt terrible. I promised her that I wouldn't smoke anymore. She and I hugged each other to seal the promise. Monday afternoon while Patch and I were waiting for the school bus, he offered me a cigarette, I took it, lit it, inhaled and exhaled, and was an outlaw again, with a smirk on my lips. On the bus, Patch and I went to the back to sit with Herbert Blevins and Botch Atkins, who carried a sharpened beer opener in his sock to defend himself against "Madison Twerps," as he called them.

I decided to switch saxophones. I put my father's smaller, shriller alto in its case, took it back over to the parlor in my grandparents' house, and stashed it behind the piano, where my father had kept it. Mr. Oliver let me use a horn that belonged to the school, an old tenor sax that was in bad shape but was larger, gutsier, jazzier than the high-pitched little alto. With Patch on his trombone, I began joining the older band members in their jam sessions before school, at lunchtime, and after school. The seniors laughed at us, they ad-libbed circles around us, but they didn't refuse our company. The band room was thick with cigarette smoke during those jam sessions, even though lots of times Mr. Oliver was sitting in his office right next door. Patch and I taught ourselves to play B-flat blues; we imitated the older kids. They were accustomed to giving each other solo breaks, to clapping, and to shouting encouraging or appreciative remarks at the soloist, the way the members of Mr. Oliver's combo did, the way the professionals did. After Patch and I had been hanging around with them for several months, they started, for a joke more than anything else, to give us solo breaks. The first time it happened, Sult Watkins pulled his trumpet away from his mouth and shouted, "Reed, baby, Reed." I was startled and stopped playing, too, but Sult shouted at me, "You, man! Play!" I was scared. I merely squawked the major chord notes while Sult and Alan Hampton, the piano player, giggled to themselves and played along with the joke of my solo. Then Sult took his break, ripped up the band room with high notes and runs and professional-sounding licks, showing me how it was supposed to be done. But Patch and I caught on, getting off by ourselves and working at it. Then I found I could do it. I sailed for days, prancing through the halls at school knowing that was something I could do, improvise a jazz break, with people all around me, clapping their hands and listening to me and shouting at me, "Go, Reed, go," while I filled up the whole huge room with sounds from my horn. I had a fancy way of sticking my cigarette into the joint of my high F-key so that it wouldn't get in my way and so that smoke curled all around my face and head while I was taking my solo breaks. Sometimes, if the light was right, I could see my reflection in the windows of the band room, and I looked exactly the way I wanted to look.

Even though it was a lot of trouble, I hauled my saxophone case around with me almost everywhere I went. The case answered most people's questions about where I was going, what I was doing. All through that year of high school, I worked to make the sound of that tenor saxophone come out in patterns and shapes and tones that were just the way I wanted them to be. Even Mr. Oliver said I'd improved since the beginning of school. He began to select me to be in smaller groups of musicians, bands to do shows and special concerts, pep bands. I began to be able to feel the horn's sound when it started in the pit of my belly, came up through my throat and mouth and teeth, through the reed and mouthpiece, down through the body of the horn and out the bell; it was like knowing that I was strong, knowing that I could lift heavy weights.

At the end of April, I got my driver's license back in the mail from Richmond. Right away I started asking for the car. My mother reminded me that I'd said I wouldn't ever want to drive again. I told her it wasn't fair of her to bring that up.

If I wasn't allowed to take the car to Madison, we had arguments at the dinner table. I'd found ways to get where I wanted to go when I hadn't had a license, had hitchhiked and bummed and begged friends to take me places. But now that I had the license, I was desperate to drive the car again. My father tried to stay out of the arguments I started, tried to let my mother make the decisions about what I could or couldn't do. But I found ways to turn everything toward him, to insist that he have the final word. He began dealing with me as if he had to be very careful not to lose his temper. He would say, "No, Reed," or "Yes, Reed," and I would know that he was thinking much more than just the small thing he was saying, would know that he was holding back.

In June, when school was out, I was restless. It was childish to be knocking on doors in Rosemary, asking ladies did they want their lawns mowed, did they want their flower beds weeded. But that was all there was to do. I stayed around the house a lot, practicing my horn (which wasn't the same all by myself) or reading, or sneaking cigarettes whenever I thought I could get away with it. Nothing was very satisfactory to me. I especially hated the nights when the whole family would watch TV, even my grandfather, who would walk over from his house in the dark to see Matt Dillon. I couldn't sit still then, would have to get up and pace into the kitchen or the study, fix something to eat, or else call Patch up to see what he was doing.

What I looked forward to was driving up to the carbide plant to pick up my father after work and seeing Darcy in her summer dresses. She came over to talk to me every day she saw me now, and I'd begun thinking a lot about her arms, which she usually crossed in front of her while she stood by the car window, and her calves and ankles, which I watched when she walked away from me. I liked to see her face, too, but I didn't think about it so much when I was away from her; her face seemed to me too cheerful and healthy to devote any time to daydreaming about. Those other parts of her body that I had seen appealed more to my outlaw self, my cigarette-smoking, jazz-playing self.

Now, when she came to the car to talk with me, Darcy would touch my elbow or catch my wrist or just put her cool hand on my arm and leave it there. Always her dresses were bright colors: yellow, blue, orange, pink, or once even white. Whenever I saw her, she was coming out of gray buildings onto a gray, dusty road. I noticed that even old sourpuss Mrs. Sharitz smiled at Darcy and waved goodbye to her at the end of the day. I could tease her a little bit, try to make her tell me who her boyfriend was, ask her when she was going out with me, things like that. Darcy claimed to be ready anytime I wanted to go out with her. I said I wanted to go out with her all the time. It was a joke, something to laugh about. I had matured enough so that I didn't mind the way the men looked at me in the car and her standing there talking to me when they walked by. One day I told Darcy they all looked the same to me, in their overalls and sweated-out shirts and carrying their dinner-buckets. I meant her to laugh about that, but she just asked me when band practice was starting up again.

On a rainy day late in June, two men from the plant, dumping a truckload of waste, were caught in a fire. There was a field some distance away where waste from the plant, mostly a gray, powdery dust, was dumped in piles. The field was locked up and marked with signs warning DANGER—KEEP OUT—NO TRESPASSING. Everybody in Rosemary knew that when carbide gets wet it generates acetylene gas, which is flammable. Boys I knew in grade school had told me that on a rainy day you could throw a rock into one of those piles where a truck had dumped the waste, and the thing would explode like in a war movie. On this day, the two men drove through the rain into the field, started to dump the load, and found themselves surrounded by fire. One man ran from the truck, through the fire, and got away with burns that would keep him in the hospital for a week or so. The other man had, in that instant of seeing the fire, decided to get under the truck to get away from it. The tires of the truck burned and went flat. The man was trapped under there until the rescue squad, the wrecking truck, a crew of men from the carbide plant, and my father could get him out. The man was conscious all that time, calling to the men who were working to get him out from under the truck.

When my father came home late in the evening, long after dark, I thought maybe he had somehow been injured himself. His color was pale gray. His skin glistened so that I could almost feel how clammy he felt. He shivered every so often. My mother fixed him a strong whiskey, and he drank that, asked for another one. She told him that she had kept supper for him. He told her he was sorry, he couldn't eat anything, he only wanted the whiskey. He wouldn't sit down. He just kept standing, shifting his weight, leaning against the mantel, so that we could see he barely had strength enough to keep on his feet. He told about it even though I was there and I knew my mother didn't want me to hear it. She didn't stop him, though. He said that the man had even been able to stand up and walk when they got him out from under the truck, but he'd been burned over most of his body. My father said that if it hadn't been for Darcy, he didn't know how any of them would have gotten through it. Darcy had made them coffee and brought it to them. Darcy had talked with them when it looked like they weren't going to be able to move the truck without killing the man underneath it. When the man's wife had come down there, Darcy had taken her away, out of the field, and quieted her, sat with her in the car. When it was all over, Darcy had driven the woman home and seen to it that she had somebody to stay with her. They didn't know if the man would live or not. They had taken him to the hospital. Finally my father went upstairs to bed. But all night long I'd wake up to hear him walking in the hallway, walking downstairs, opening and shutting doors. I'd see the hall light on and his shadow moving past my doorway.

For a long while after that accident I didn't like to see my father. His face was drawn. He looked at me with such a desperate expression that I thought he wanted something from me. I didn't know what it was. He lost his appetite, lost weight. Even while he sat at his desk in the study, with his back to me, I couldn't look at him without thinking of the fire in the field and the burned man. It changed how I thought about Darcy, too. I couldn't put together what my father had said about her with the vision I had of her, a pretty girl who liked to joke around with me about dating. For almost the whole month of July, I didn't go up to the carbide plant.

My birthday was not celebrated that year. Mother gave me a check my father had written out that morning before he went to work. The burned man had died during the night.

Patch had gotten some music from Mr. Oliver that we could work on, some duets for trombone and saxophone, and a couple of a little dance-band arrangements. We started practicing over at his house. Usually his mother wasn't around. We smoked cigarettes right in his living room while we played. Patch offered me one of his father's beers from the refrigerator. I took it and drank it as if I were used to having a beer on a hot afternoon. Patch didn't make the offer but just that once;

I think he might have had to account to his father for the missing beer. One afternoon when I was working under a hot August sun to weed Mrs. Peacock's pachysandra beds, Patch came running up there to tell me the news: Mr. Oliver had called him and told him that, starting that fall, he wanted both of us to be in his combo. We would have to start going to Madison right away to practice and learn the numbers. Patch and I yelled a lot and congratulated each other there in Mrs. Peacock's yard. I threw a dirt clod at him. Mrs. Peacock came out and said she thought I'd done enough for that day, how much did she owe me. I walked Patch home. Then he walked me home, both of us talking, neither one of us listening to the other one. We'd get paid for playing in that combo. We were going to be professionals.

Patch went with me in the car to the carbide plant. I surprised Mother by asking if I could go up there that afternoon. I thought taking Patch to see Darcy when she came out would be a fine way for us to celebrate. We were so jazzy. We sang be-bop riffs at each other in the car while I drove and while we sat waiting for the whistle to blow quitting time. I didn't tell Patch anything about Darcy. I wanted her coming over to the car to be a real surprise to him.

When Darcy came out of the gatehouse, she had on a bright blue dress, and her hair was down around her shoulders, but she kept her eyes on the ground, and she looked sad in a way that I'd never seen her look. I figured that walking that way she wouldn't even notice the car sitting there. So I called out to her, "Hey, Darcy," maybe a little too loud and casual. But she just lifted her head enough to glance at me and say "Hi." Didn't even say "Hi, Reed," didn't even use my name. And kept on walking. The last couple of steps to her car she ran, taking quick little steps in her high-heeled shoes. The whistle blew just about the time Patch asked me who she was. I said, "Oh, that's Darcy," like she wasn't anybody special to me.

My father came out but wouldn't take the passenger seat in front that Patch offered him, just sat in the back, studying his dinner-bucket, and wouldn't say much to either one of us. When I drove Patch to his house and let him out, my father still wouldn't come up to the front seat. I got after him to tell me what the matter was. I was still pestering him when we came into the kitchen, I don't know why. I was kidding with him, trying to cheer him up, but in another way I was trying to dig at him, get him mad. While he was washing his hands and trying to talk with my mother, I was still asking him questions. Then he lost his temper. He told me to get the hell away from him just for a few minutes. I went into the living room and listened to my mother ask him what was wrong while he was drying his hands. He let the silence stretch out for a while. I heard Mother go back to what she was doing at the stove; I guessed she'd decided she wasn't going to get an answer from him. Then he told her, "Bernard Oglesby and Mrs. Oglesby and Darcy."

My mother said, "What?"

He said, "Would you like to see the letter?"

Mother said that she would. I heard him digging in his pocket for it. Then he went into his study. I could hear both of them being quiet while she read the letter in the kitchen. She carried it into the study to give it back to him and said, "Oh."

I piped up from the living room, "I want to see it, too."

Mother said, "No."

My father said, "Yes, damn it, he wants to have his nose in my business. I want him to see it."

So I came in and picked the letter up off his desk and read it. It was written in sixth- or seventh-grade handwriting, on

lined note-tablet paper. It was addressed to my father, Mr.
Bryant. In it Mrs. Oglesby began by saying that Bernard had
always spoken highly of my father. She said that Bernard
thought my father was a fair man. She was just wondering if
my father couldn't do something about the woman who had
got Bernard so upset. Bernard was not able to pay attention
to his family or do much of anything after work except go
and buy Pabst Blue Ribbon Beer at Miss Tessie's filling station
and take their family car and go ride around on the dirt roads
of Mercy County. Mrs. Oglesby said that my father knew
what woman she was talking about, she didn't have to call
any names.

I whistled when I finished the letter. I set it back on my
father's desk, right in front of him. But he swiveled his chair
around to face me.

"Now," my father said, and gave me a look that was both
angry and beseeching, "what would you do?"

"I don't know," I said.

"What did you do?" my mother called from the kitchen.

"I showed it to Darcy," he said. He was talking to Mother
in the kitchen, but he was looking at me while he spoke.
"She said that occasionally she speaks to Bernard Oglesby in
the morning when she comes in to work, but she doesn't
ever see him anytime except then. She said he stands by
his car and tips his hat to her when she walks past him in
the mornings."

"And then what did you do?" my mother asked, coming
to the door of the study to be able to see him. We were both
looking at him hard, feeling sorry for him but deadly curious
at the same time.

"I showed the letter to Bernard Oglesby. Bernard said that
he would take care of it this evening at home. I told him that
if I heard of him lifting a hand against his wife, I would fire

him. I told him that if I had any further reports of his drinking beer and driving around Mercy County in the vicinity of Preacher Webster's house, I would fire him. He said he didn't think that was fair. I told him I didn't give a damn about what he thought was fair, that was what I was going to do. Fire him. And he said all right."

"That's all?" my mother asked.

"That's all," he said.

When school started again that fall, Patch and I were members of the Mellowtones, a professional musical organization that played for dances in Virginia, West Virginia, Tennessee, and North Carolina. The other members of the band were Mr. Oliver on trumpet; Mr. Chambers, the band director from Oakley, on piano; Dr. Kahn, a dentist in Madison, on bass fiddle; and Mr. Webb, who ran a hardware store in Max Meadows, on drums. That quartet played all the numbers; Patch and I joined in, to add saxophone and trombone, on about half of them. He and I each had one solo number. Patch's was "Night and Day"; mine was "Love Letters in the Sand." We were paid half of what the other members of the band were paid. The Mellowtones worked a heavy schedule through the winter, Patch and I sometimes getting to bed only a couple of hours before sunrise during the Christmas and New Year's season. We did a lot of traveling with those men, always riding in Dr. Kahn's station wagon, Patch and I talking to him, keeping him awake while the others slept. The men assumed we both smoked, which we did. They told us dirty jokes, kidded us about girls. They looked the other way if Patch and I decided to accept a drink when we were offered one by somebody at a dance. We were surprised that it happened almost everywhere we played. But then we figured out that people who went to dances thought that people—even boys like us—who played in bands were immoral persons. Patch started wearing sunglasses so he would look less like a freckle-faced kid from Rosemary and more like a depraved jazzman.

Patch already had a notion of who was going to offer us a drink at the Soiree Club Annual Dance at the Madison Country Club. It was April again, we'd been several weeks without playing anywhere, and the members of the Soiree Club brought in with them through the doors gales of laughter, strong wafts of perfume and cologne, armloads of brown bags with bottles in them. Most of them were middle-aged people, doing the old-style dances, singing along with "Stardust" and "I'll Get By" and "Blue Skies," requesting "Sweet Georgia Brown" every set. They were folks who stood out on the dance floor in groups of six or eight, clasping each other, shouting and laughing between numbers. Sitting over in a corner, not dancing or talking with any of the others, was a couple who were friends of Patch's parents. Patch said they were real hell-raisers. They were giving him winks, lifting their glasses to him, clapping loudly after everything we played. Patch said they were getting loaded. Patch said at the end of the next break we'd go over to talk to them and see what happened.

Darcy came in. I half stood up to go meet her. I forgot for a moment that I had a horn strapped around my neck, that I wore the powder-blue-and-navy dinner jacket of a Mellowtone, that I was on the bandstand behind microphones, mutes, speakers, and lighted music stands. Darcy looked better than anyone there. She stood, unbuttoning her coat, smiling a little, and in the soft light of the room her skin was tanned, her hair a light shade of brown and shiny, held back behind her shoulders with a dangling yellow ribbon. A lull came in the noise. For a moment it looked like she had come to the dance by herself. But then a sandy-haired man in a dark suit stepped through the door behind her. When he closed the door and turned, he saw most of the people standing on the dance floor and sitting at the tables staring at the place where he and Darcy stood. The color of his face went darker.

We were about to start "How High the Moon," in which Patch and I had to play the opening eight bars. Mr. Oliver counted off by tapping his foot loudly, *one, two*. I held my horn ready and watched the man point Darcy over toward one of the side rooms. We startled the people out on the floor with the first notes of the number. Everyone began dancing, but I could still see the man helping Darcy off with her coat, see that her yellow dress came down in the back to below her shoulder blades. Mr. Oliver pointed his trumpet at me, blew "How High the Moon" right straight at me, and looked hard at me over the bell of his horn. Patch elbowed me and said, "He wants us to clap. He's been trying to get your attention."

I started to clap while Mr. Oliver stood up and ad-libbed his solo. Usually I enjoyed clapping while the rest of the combo played, but with Darcy there I felt stupid doing it. Even that was better than what we did on Latin American numbers. On cha-chas and rumbas, Patch beat on a cowbell with a drumstick, and I thwacked one ebony woodblock against another in a cadence that was sort of like *shave-and-a-haircut—two bits*. I always felt dumb doing that. I saw that Darcy was paying attention only to the sandy-haired man. He did everything he was supposed to do, checked their coats, found them a table, brought over a bottle of mixer, fixed their drinks, put the liquor bottle in its brown paper bag on the floor under their table, spoke to the people around them, shook hands, introduced Darcy. But he wasn't right for her. He had no grace or ease. You could see how much effort everything he did was costing him, as if having a good time were hard work.

Darcy, however, looked like she'd done nothing all her life but go to parties, enjoy herself, and make the people around her smile at her. Once I heard her laugh above all the other noise in the room; it made me smile while I was clapping. Then it was time for Patch and me to play the closing riffs. Riffs were fast little complicated variations on the melody, be-bop arrangements; we sounded like trumpet, sax, and trombone were improvising in perfect harmony. When we smacked those first, crisp notes, the sound picked up volume and energy. People turned their heads to watch us. I saw Darcy just then recognize me for the first time, saw her face brighten, knew she was glad to see me. Mr. Oliver took his trumpet away from his mouth just long enough to shout at me, "Settle down!" I calmed down then and played evenly. When we finished the number, Mr. Oliver grinned at me and said, "What's wrong with you, Reed?" He didn't want an answer.

We played "Stars Fell on Alabama," and almost everyone came out on the floor to dance, including Darcy and the sandy-haired man. They were exactly the same height when they danced, Darcy talking with him almost nose to nose. She gave me a big smile. I knew she was telling him about me. I saw him look at me a couple of times, saw him set his jaw and listen while she talked.

When we finished, Darcy led him over to the bandstand; she came directly to me and said, "Hello, Mr. Music Man." She introduced me to Phil. Then I tried to introduce Darcy and Phil to the others. It got awkward until they all just told each other their names. Phil shook hands with Mr. Oliver, but he only waved to the others, which was the right thing to do. We were still in the set, not taking a break. Darcy asked Mr. Oliver if he would let me off the bandstand long enough to dance with her. Mr. Oliver assured her that he would, next set or the one after that. When they walked back to their table, I saw Patch studying Darcy's back and shoulders the same as I was. He clapped me on the knee and said, "Hey, man." Then Mr. Oliver said we'd play "Night and Day," Patch's solo, for the last number of the set. Patch said, "Man, I'm going to blow them right out of their shoes." And he did. Standing up there, leaning back, with his eyes closed, he played the smoothest, gutsiest "Night and Day" any of us had ever heard out of him. I played the woodblocks, and Mr. Oliver shook the maracas. When it was over, all of us in the band applauded Patch, who was red-faced, sweating, and delighted with himself.

At the break I saw Darcy and Phil signaling me to come to their table. "See you later, 'Night and Day,' " I said to Patch. I was too aware of myself walking across the empty dance floor. Darcy was holding a chair for me, and I took it, beside her but across the table from Phil.

"Oh, Reed, I think you're really good." She beamed at me. I took off my glasses to clean them, hoping that would keep me from looking too smug. Phil chimed in with, "Pretty good sound there, boy." He was putting ice in a glass, fixing a drink. I asked Darcy how she liked my woodblock-playing. She didn't understand the sarcasm. I explained how I hated the woodblocks. She looked vague. "But they add to the music," she said. Phil handed me the drink. I took it, sipped it, tasted bourbon. I made an effort not to look surprised and said, "Thanks, Phil." I told them about the men in the band, who was who and what kind of work they did, but Darcy was the only one who listened. Phil kept looking around the room, even when Darcy tried to draw him into the conversation. She told me that Phil was just starting out with his own contracting business and that he went to dances all the time, in Roanoke and Bristol and all around. "You think Reed's band is as good as any you've heard, don't you, Phil?" she said.

"Sure do," Phil said, craning his neck to look around behind him.

Before I went back to the bandstand, I thanked Phil again for the drink. He told me that there were some people he had to talk to later on; he hoped I would be able to keep Darcy company while he did it. He gave me a grin and a wink. Darcy said, "Oh, poor Reed, he'll never be able to stand being with me by himself." It was our old joke, at the car window outside the gatehouse at the carbide plant. I laughed with her and mumbled that I thought I could handle it.

The next set was going to take us through midnight. Mr. Oliver explained to me that he'd let me have the last two numbers off to dance with Darcy. I asked him to make them slow numbers because I couldn't dance to anything fast. He laughed at me, said he'd thought I was a real be-bopper, he was disappointed in me. But he went ahead and put two slow ones at the end of the set. Patch smelled my breath and gave me the lifted eyebrows, which I thought was very juvenile of him. He whispered to me, "Nothing but ginger ale. I sat over there, listened to those two old birds the whole break. They gave me nothing but ginger ale." I told him that ginger ale was what a young fellow like him was supposed to drink. We played a good set: "Ain't Misbehaving," "Mood Indigo," "Tea for Two," "Cherokee," and "Woodchopper's Ball," in which I got a couple of solo breaks. I imagined that the bourbon had made me looser. I paid attention to how the whole band sounded, and I thought I played solidly. Mr. Oliver nodded at me, and then it was time for me to step off the bandstand while the others stayed up there. I could feel them watching me when I walked away from them.

"Here he is," Phil said when I came up to their table, and I thought he might have meant to be sarcastic, but I didn't pay any attention to him. I asked Darcy would she like to dance, and because it was something to do with my hands, I held her chair while she came out to the floor. Phil got up, too. "Have fun, kids," he said; he started making his way back through the tables toward the Players' Lounge where some of the older men had gathered to smoke cigars and talk. "Moonlight in Vermont," one of the numbers Mr. Oliver sang, was the first one Darcy and I danced to. I was nervous about touching her, about starting my feet moving, but it was easy after the first couple of steps. I decided everything was logical: music, dancing, having Darcy that close to me, having my arm around her waist, her arm around my shoulder. "You smell great," I said. Then I decided that was a crude thing to say. "I'm sorry," I said. Darcy gave me a light tap with her hand on my back and moved her forehead so that it touched the side of my chin. I felt my blood moving up through my body toward my head. "Tell me about your music," she said. "Not about those others." She motioned the hand I was holding over toward the band. "Just you."

"Like what?" I said. I matched my tone with hers, low and soft, as if we knew each other better than we actually did.

"Like how you got started," she said. "You know."

I stammered a little getting started, but then words started spilling out of my mouth. I told her about my father's old alto saxophone, stashed in behind the piano over at my grandparents' house, how he'd had it overhauled and put in perfect condition before he packed it away and started work at the carbide plant. Darcy was surprised that my father had played at all. I told her that he'd been very good, that he'd had his own orchestra in Rosemary back in the old days, had taught each person in it how to play his instrument. I told her about the picture in the study at home, of my father with his band, the two women in long, formal-looking dresses sitting at the piano, the solemn-faced men in dark jackets and white-duck pants sitting, holding their instruments in their laps, banjo, clarinet, trumpet, guitar, and my father standing up with his saxophone held in front of him.

"And he taught you, too?" she asked.

I told her that he had, that it had been hard for him because I was always getting ahead of him, learning things before I was supposed to but not practicing the things he wanted me to work on.

"Your father thinks you have a lot of ability," Darcy said. "Moonlight in Vermont" was coming to an end.

"You mean I make good grades in school?" I had to shout the question at her because everyone on the dance floor was applauding. "Thank you, thank you very much," Mr. Oliver said into the microphone. We wandered back toward Darcy's table, but Phil wasn't there, and so we didn't sit down. Darcy picked up her glass and sipped. "Want the rest?" she said. I took the glass and emptied it. She was frowning. "I think he meant more than just grades in school," she said.

The Mellowtones started playing "Laura," which Mr. Oliver knew was one of my favorite songs, one that he had asked me not to sing along with; he said that my voice had not matured enough for me to be much of a singer yet. Darcy and I went out among the other couples on the dance floor. We held each other and swayed to that slow ballad, our feet barely moving. She let her forehead rest against my shoulder. My vision closed down to just Darcy and me and the soft light around us. When it was over, Darcy said, "I could use some air." I said that I could, too, and I wasn't kidding; I felt like I'd been holding my breath for a long time. We strolled out onto the patio balcony. I felt the cool air sweep across the sweat on my forehead, and I was grateful for it. "What about Phil?" I asked her.

"He's a big boy," she said.

Other couples were there outside, some of them smoking. I took out the pack of Chesterfields I'd bought for Patch and me for the night. "I don't want one," she said, "and I don't want you to have one either." She took the cigarette out of my hand and dropped it over the railing. "Can we walk some here?" she asked. She put her arm lightly around my waist then, and I put mine around her bare shoulders. I was pretty impressed with myself for doing that. We headed for the steps that led off the balcony and down onto the golf course. It was too dark to see at first, but then we got used to being out of the light. The farther out into the dark field we walked, the more clearly we could see each other. Darcy's skin was gray, and her dress had become white, moon-colored. In her high-heeled shoes, it was difficult for her to walk. She leaned against me while we went slowly up a hill toward the dark shapes of trees. "You're lucky to have a father who has some respect for you," she said. "Mine doesn't think I have a brain in my head."

"I always imagined your father as a big man with heavy shoulders, thick, bushy eyebrows, and a loud bass voice," I told her. "Preacher Webster from Mercy County. I can almost see him on horseback, riding to turn sinners into Methodists," I said.

Darcy laughed. "No," she said. "My father's not as tall as I am, he's been bald ever since I can remember, and he has a soft voice. When I'm home, he follows me around from room to room, giving me advice, asking me what I'm going to do, offering to help me."

"So what do you do?" I asked her.

"Tell him that I'm a grown woman." I could feel her shivering, and because I'd seen Nelson Eddy do it for Jeannette MacDonald in the movies, I took off my jacket and put it over Darcy's shoulders. "Thank you." she said. She put her arm back around my waist while we walked. "I tell him that I appreciate his care for me but that I have my own life."

"What effect does that have on him?"

She laughed again. "None whatsoever. He says, 'Yes, Darcy, but,' and then keeps following me around advising and counseling."

"I don't think my father knows anything about my life," I said. I hadn't thought about it before, but it seemed true when I said it. We walked without saying anything for a while. Then Darcy spoke just as we reached the shadow of the trees.

"He'd surprise you with what he knows, Reed."

We both stopped walking and then stood like we were dancing in the shadow of the trees out there on the grass. We were both shivering. "You're wrong," I said.

"All right," she said. She headed us back toward the lighted windows of the country club. I was glad to be going back because I was cold.

"Will Phil be mad?" I asked her when we came to the steps.

"No," she said. "He's somebody I used to know a long time ago. He doesn't care what I do here."

I followed her up the steps. "You mean you don't know him anymore," I said. She stopped and turned around. I came up to face-level with her. She let me kiss her, but she didn't seem especially interested in it, just rested her hands on my shoulders.

"You know what I mean," she said. When we came up on the balcony, she handed me back my jacket. I put it on, and we went inside. I followed her to the table, helped her with her chair, sat down beside her. Phil wasn't anywhere to be seen.

"Do you want me to fix you a drink?" I asked.

"No," she said. She stared at the small candle-flame sputtering in its blue glass jar in the center of the table.

"Well," I said. But I couldn't think of anything else to say. I took off my glasses, cleaned them, put them back on, and watched the people in the room. Patch came up to tell me it was time to get back on the stand. I didn't want to leave Darcy there by herself, but she told me to go ahead, she'd find Phil. Up on the bandstand I got some fishy looks from Mr. Webb and Dr. Kahn. Mr. Oliver said, "O.K., young stud, let's see if you can get through 'Love Letters in the Sand.' " I thought I was playing my solo as well as Patch had played his. I didn't look out onto the dance floor, or anywhere except down at my music stand. I wanted to imagine how Darcy would look while she listened to me play. But when I opened my eyes at the end, I didn't see her anywhere. People out on the floor applauded, but the guys in the band didn't act like I had played it any better than I usually did. During the next number, I saw Phil with Darcy, getting their coats. I was playing then, going through some hard riffs in "Somewhere There's Music." At the door Darcy just lifted a hand to wave. She was wearing what I thought was a sad kind of smile when she went out with Phil.

It was the following Wednesday before I had a chance to drive the car up to the carbide plant. That afternoon, Darcy and my father came out of the gatehouse together, talking. They stood right beside me at the car window and discussed a report that my father kept insisting had to be gotten to New York right away. I watched him kick dust in the road while they stood there. Darcy didn't look once at me. Then, when she said goodbye to my father, she turned to me as if she were seeing me for the first time and gave me a wonderful smile. I said hello, and I was starting to ask her how she'd liked the party Saturday night, but she was saying goodbye, turning, and going toward her own car. On the way home I hoped my father would say something that would provoke me so that I could start an argument with him or say something hateful to him. But he sat quietly, looking out at the river, not much interested in talking with me.

One Saturday in mid-May, after a long marching-band practice, Patch and I pulled into the parking lot of the High Hat, and Darcy was there. First I noticed her car, and then I saw that she was in it, sitting behind the wheel, by herself. I asked Patch to back his father's car up beside hers so that I could talk with her out my window. The afternoon was bright, and I couldn't tell if Darcy was trying to smile at me or just squinting from the sun when she saw me. She said "Hi, Reed," and she asked me how I was doing. I got out of Patch's car and perched up on its front fender to make conversation with her. Something was wrong with her, something darkened about her face. She lit a cigarette. I told her I didn't know she smoked.

"Sometimes, when I'm in the mood, I do," she said. She offered me one, and I took it, clamped it between my teeth when I lit it. I asked her what she'd been doing. She shook her head like she didn't want to answer. Then she said, "Driving around, sitting out here, thinking."

"Problems?" I asked her.

"Nothing that won't go away of its own accord," she said.

I didn't like to think of her sitting there in her car by herself. I looked around the parking lot, which was empty except for two other cars. Even on a bright afternoon, this was an ugly place to be spending time. The High Hat Drive-In was a flat, squat building with Pepsi Cola signs and neon lights all over it. The place was right on the edge of Madison where the highway traffic was almost always heavy. "You want to go inside with Patch and me to get something to eat?" I asked her.

Darcy threw her cigarette out the window, shook her head, and ran her fingers through her hair. "Sure," she said, in a forced kind of way, as if she were determined to get herself in a better frame of mind.

Patch swung himself out of the car and hitched up his pants. "We're going inside and act like we're used to coming to the city," he said.

"You miserable hick," I said.

When Darcy got out of the car, I saw that she was wearing dungarees, loafers, and white socks. Her blouse wasn't even tucked in. She stuck her hands in her pockets, trying to give me a big smile, but it didn't work for her. Her face lapsed into an expression that was half getting ready to cry and half frowning. She watched the asphalt under her feet while we were walking to the door of the High Hat. I told her I'd never seen her in dungarees. I told her she looked good.

"Thanks, Reed," she said. She touched my arm and then let it go, which I took to mean that she appreciated my good intentions but she saw through my flattery. Patch bowed and opened the door for us. Inside was a line of booths on the highway side of the building, all of them empty, and on the other side a counter with a line of stools on one of which sat a waitress reading the paper and sipping coffee.

"Table for three, please," Patch said, coming up behind us. The waitress gave him a short look over the top of her glasses, jerked her head back toward the booths, and said, "Any one you want, Son."

Patch took one side of a booth; Darcy and I took the other. He was fidgety, took out his change and spread it on the table in front of him. After the waitress had taken our orders, Patch got up to play the jukebox. Both Darcy and I gave him money to put in for us. He stayed up there in front of the machine a long time, feeding quarters into it, punching buttons. I asked Darcy what was wrong. I told her I wasn't used to seeing her in a bad mood.

She shook her head again. "Take my mind off it, Reed. Talk to me. Tell me something."

I thought hard. Everything I could think of to say was dull. "I haven't done anything fascinating recently," I said.

Patch came back and sat down, humming along with the Everly Brothers' "Bird Dog" from the jukebox. The silence hung over the table. Finally he said, "Something going on out there on that highway that I can't see?" He kept shifting his position in the booth, singing along with the songs on the jukebox, patting on the table with his hands. The waitress watched him grimly when she brought our chiliburgers and French fries and milkshakes and Darcy's coffee. Patch and I ate. After that it was easier to talk. Patch said something about how he wished the Mellowtones could play some newer music, and I agreed with him. It was an old subject for us, but we kept it going to try to perk up Darcy. Patch sang his rendition of "Peggy Sue" and got a smile from her. I was aware that I was trying to please her with my talk, describing things in funny ways, using special words. Patch gave me a couple of odd looks while I was speaking. After a while he stopped saying much. I kept trying to get him back in the conversation, but all he would say was "Yeah, that's right," or "O.K., man." Then we were all three quiet. "Saturday afternoon," Patch said and sighed and slapped the table. Darcy asked the waitress for another cup of coffee. After she'd gotten it and was sipping it, Patch said "Saturday afternoon" again. The jukebox ran out of songs. We sat there looking out the window at cars passing on the highway. Patch said he thought he ought to be going. I asked him what was his hurry. He said he wasn't in any real hurry. He'd been having a fantastic time all afternoon, he said, but he thought he could find a better way to spend his Saturday night than to sit over a table full of dirty dishes and watch the flies.

Darcy was smoking then. She was down to the bottom of her cup of coffee. She said, as much into her cup as to me, "Let him go ahead. I'll take you home." So I told Patch to go ahead, I'd see him Monday. He stood up and did a little dance to shake his pegged pants down his legs. He bowed to us. "I'll see you children later," he said. "Be careful in the big city." I felt strange sending him out like that, seeing him go off without me. After he'd driven out of the parking lot, Darcy and I talked about him. I told her Patch had been in the wreck with me. She said that my father hadn't said much about it to her or to anybody up at the carbide plant. So I told her about the wreck. I said a few things about Bobby Sloan that made Darcy laugh, about him saying "Thank you, Jesus," and being too fat to crawl out the car window. I went on talking about Bobby, told her how he represented everything bad that the Madison kids thought about people from Rosemary. "Except you said he was smart," Darcy said. She seemed more her old self.

"That's right," I said, "but he isn't really even that smart. He just studies all the time."

Darcy took up for Bobby Sloan, and I didn't mind. At least we had a conversation going. We watched it go gray outside and then deeper and deeper shades of blue. The waitress came to clear away our dishes, made us squeeze away from the table while she wiped with a gray cloth. People began coming in and talking loudly. "Want to go drive around some?" Darcy asked. "No law that says you have to stay in one place while you're waiting out your troubles." I was glad to be outside with her in the warm evening air. I stretched until my bones cracked. While we were walking toward her car, she handed me her keys.

"You trust me?" I asked her.

She just looked at me and went around to the passenger side of her car. It had been partially customized and was kind of a hot rod; she had told me before, in our carbide plant quitting-time conversations, that her brother worked on it for her. I had teased her about it then, told her I thought she was one of those Mercy County bootleggers, asked her did she know the words to "Thunder Road." When I started up that old Mercury, the exhaust noise was deafening until I let up on the accelerator. Darcy grinned and said she was sure I would get used to it.

We drove through town, up around the schoolhouse, then out to the Madison Country Club, which was locked up and dark except for a small light back in the kitchen. I pulled up in front of the front door and beeped the horn.

"Why'd you do that?" Darcy asked.

"Always beep your horn in front of a dark building," I said. I turned out the lights but kept the car idling. "I'm not so bad driving a straight shift, am I?"

Darcy said that I was terrible. We both fiddled with the radio to see if we could find music that suited us. When we were leaning forward together like that, her hair made a small tent for our faces. I told her that I liked her hair down like that. She switched the radio off.

"Come on, Reed. I don't need that kind of cheering up anymore," she said. "Let's get out of here before somebody thinks we're trying to break into this place."

"You don't want to take another walk on the golf course?" I asked her. She said she didn't.

We drove back to the schoolhouse. Every window in it was dark except for the exit signs at the doors. "The Old Schoolhouse," I said. I steered the car up over the curb and onto the sidewalk. I drove slowly all the way down the length of the building, past the band room, all the classrooms, the principal's office, the gymnasium, and the cafeteria. Then I drove back down over the curb into the teachers' parking lot. But Darcy was quiet the whole time, didn't even giggle. I didn't say anything about it either. At first I'd been proud of myself for thinking of such a droll thing, but then I decided it was childish and disgusting.

I headed us out the back way from town, as if I were going to Gantley the long way. When I saw Fish Hatchery Road, I turned off there and went along that dirt road slowly until we came to the fish hatchery. I turned in, stopped the car in the empty parking lot, turned out the lights, and turned the engine off. I did these things as they came to me to do; I did not plan them. The place was dark and full of frog noises. It smelled like water. Darcy opened the door like she'd been waiting for me to get her just exactly to that stopping place. I got out, too, and followed her.

It was warm out. There was no wind. In the dark I could make out Darcy, her hair hiding her face, just strolling across the parking lot toward the walkways and paths that led to the trout pools. Trees were all around us, mostly willows; they made it look like any direction we turned we would be heading into a wall of darkness. What light there was came down from the moon and stars; the trees scattered it like sunlight in patches on the ground. In the daytime, you could see trout in those pools, divided according to size, packed in so that the water was thick with them. In the daylight, you could see the markings on their sides, the light stripes of pink stippling on the rainbows, the red flecks on the brook trout. But now, in the dark, we could see only a yawning black rectangle that represented a pool, then white foam when the water was stirred up as we walked past each one. We could hear, even above the constant sound of fast-running water, the sound of water being thrashed and churned by fish.

Darcy and I passed along the tree-lined walkways, past half a dozen trout pools, until we came to the small park down at the very end, away from the main building and the parking lot. An area of smooth grass was surrounded by trees and benches. On one side was a small pool where only the largest trout were kept just for visitors to see and feed if they wanted to. Darcy stood over that pool, bending over and staring into the water. When she gestured toward it with her hand, the water made a sound like an engine picking up speed, and the surface of it became a white froth. "Those trout can take a finger off," I said to her. She looked at me over her shoulder, but she didn't say anything.

I sat down on a bench and waited to see what she would do. After a while she came slowly over and sat beside me. It was very dark. We sat close to each other, peering into each other's faces. I took off my glasses. "It doesn't make any difference," I said. "I can see you the same with them off or with them on." I spoke up loudly so that my voice would carry over the sound of rushing water. Darcy looked around us, at the dark trees, the patches of light on the ground. Over one of the pools, we could see mist rising in a shaft of soft blue light. "We could be under the sea, Reed. We could be at the very bottom of the ocean," she said. She stood up and took both my hands and raised me up with her. We went out onto the grass where there was an open spot of light coming down. We stood under the light and put our arms around each other, rocked and took slow steps, turning ourselves in a circle.

Darcy squeezed me hard, and I lifted her chin to kiss her. I was the one who kissed her, but she kissed back hard, opened her mouth to me, and pressed against me. We lay down on the grass together, pushing our mouths and teeth together, panting through our noses. Darcy pressed against me with her whole body and held me with more strength than I'd imagined she would have. We couldn't get close enough to each other, couldn't touch each other enough. I fumbled at the buttons of her blouse, she trying to help but getting in the way, finally both of us getting it open and the brassiere unclasped in the back. She pushed it up over her breasts and pulled me down. We were like two people fighting with each other, pulling at each other with our hands, breathing so hard we were snorting. Then I undid the button and unzipped the zipper of Darcy's dungarees, and it all stopped. Darcy took her arms away from me and lay back on the grass, catching her breath. I scooted closer to her and put my hand on her belly. Darcy kept her arms still beside her. She looked past my shoulder at the sky.

I pushed closer to her, but she stayed quiet. She was breathing very calmly. "Will you do this with me?" I asked her.

"Yes," Darcy said after a long while. "Yes, if you want to."

"Don't you want to?" I said. I sat up and began to tug at her dungarees and her underpants, wanting to help her get them off. Darcy lifted her hips as I tugged, but she didn't move her hands to help me.

"No," she said.

I had her pants in a tangle at her thighs. In the light, her skin was the color of my grandmother's bone-china dinner plates, a length of smooth whiteness up to her unbuttoned blouse and loosened brassiere. I stopped pulling at her clothes.

"You don't want to," I said.

"Yes, that's right," she answered evenly.

"But you will anyway?" I asked.

"Yes," she said again, "if you want to," softly, neutrally.

I sat beside her there on the grass, in the pale light, looking at her for a long time. She lay still, watching me. The shape of her body, her breasts, the narrowing of her trunk from her hips to her waist, was the shape of a woman I thought I had dreamed. I put my hand on Darcy's ribs and then her belly again. Even then I wasn't certain either one of us was there with the other one. I stared at her so long that we both were floating, were being carried downstream in a heave of dark water. I shook my head. "All right," I said. I took my hand off her and put it on myself. I ached.

Darcy stood up then, used my shoulder to help balance herself. She slid the clump of pants, underpants, and socks down off her legs, took off the blouse and the brassiere, let them fall to the ground, and shook out her hair with her hands. Then she shook her arms and her legs like an animal shaking off rain. One piece at a time, she put her clothes back on, the underpants, the brassiere, the blouse, the dungarees, and finally her shoes. She picked up the socks and held them like she didn't know what to do with them. She muttered something about socks, I couldn't hear exactly what it was.

"What?" I said. I was unbuckling my pants, trying to get my underwear rearranged and my shirttail tucked in.

"Don't like them," she said, walking away from me, twirling the socks one in each hand. I walked over to the bench and recovered my glasses. When I looked back at Darcy, she was standing beside the pool, bending a little, dangling one of the socks up over the water. There was a whooshing burst up out of the water, a pipelike shape the size of the thick part of a man's arm. Darcy jumped back from the pool. The sock was gone from her hand. The water was churning as if someone had thrown a running outboard motor into it. Darcy hadn't made a sound, but when I came up beside her I could tell she'd been scared. The big trout continued to roil in the water, and though I couldn't see it, I imagined they had ripped that sock to shreds. "Those fools think it's food," I said.

"It's just my dumb sock," Darcy said. Then she saw she was holding the other one in her hand. She leaned forward and dropped that one in the pool, too. Again there came more splashing and thumping. "I bet they all get sick and die," she said. I hugged her shoulders, and she put her arms around my waist. We headed back to the parking lot, bumping our hips against each other as we went. When we came out of the little park, we saw the figure of a man standing stark still in the dark near one of the pools of smaller fish. "Damn!" Darcy said in a whisper. "Damn him!"

"Did you get an eyeful?" I called out at the shadow, but it made no sound. It gave no sign of life.

We were shivering when we got back to the car.

The next day was Sunday. I expected Darcy would be in church that morning, listening to her father preach. The thought of that made me smile to myself while I sat in our church with my father and mother. That afternoon I called Darcy. Her mother said that she was taking a nap, could I call back. When I called back, her father, in a thin, high-pitched voice, said that she and her mother had gone up to Gantley and wouldn't be back until late.

Monday I drove the car up to the plant. Darcy came out of the gatehouse and waved to me, gave me a smile, but she walked straight to her car. I started to call out to her, but I was too embarrassed to do it in front of the men who walked all around her heading toward their cars and trucks. I called her house that night. Her mother said she'd gone out with some young people from the church. She didn't know when Darcy would be back.

Tuesday in school, through civics, algebra, and study hall, I wrote Darcy a letter. In the beginning of it my tone was angry; at the end of it I told her that I couldn't think about anything or anybody else except her. I said that I felt a great pressure of things I wanted to say to her, things I wanted to hear her say back to me. I apologized to her for my aggressive behavior. I said that I thought she could trust me from now on. I told her that if Bernard Oglesby was following her around, I was certain I could get my father to make him stop. I mailed the letter and didn't call her, didn't go up to the carbide plant all that week. I didn't get a letter back. I didn't hear anything from her.

I fell into a mood that surprised even me. In classes I found myself being noisy and as fresh with my teachers as any of the very worst of the boys from Rosemary ever were. Mrs. Yerkes, my algebra teacher, sent me to the principal's office two days in a row. Tall, pale Mrs. Lancaster, my English teacher, who sometimes had to leave the classroom because of migraine headaches and who praised my book reports, kept me after school to ask what had gotten into me. I didn't know, I told her, and that wasn't really a lie, because even though I knew that the way I felt had to do with Darcy, I didn't know exactly how it worked. Part of it was that since I couldn't see her or talk with her, I became less and less certain that it had happened, that we had gone with each other to that place. It was like a dream I'd had that was being taken away from me. Mrs. Lancaster gave me a long, kindly look and did not break the silence of the room for a while. I fiddled with my glasses and stared at the names scratched in the wooden desk where I sat: POTTSIE II, JANET, and GUTHRIE THE OGRE. Mrs. Lancaster said that she hoped my conduct would improve. She said that whether or not I liked it, I was an example to many of the other Rosemary students who attended Madison High School. She said there were only six of us from Rosemary who were in the College Preparatory Program. After each thing she told me, I said "Yes, ma'am." Finally she let me go out of the empty classroom.

But I didn't like being an example. I was at my worst on the school bus, with the others from Rosemary. I didn't like being thought of as different from them; I was one of them. I joined the school-bus fighting, which, as a good student, I'd always tried to stay out of. I'd had my ears gouged, my ribs thunked, my head slapped, and then turned around to see Herbert or George or Botch or Elmo Blair staring innocently out the window. Now I became a gouger, thunker, head-slapper. I joined the others in harassing the freshmen and eighth-graders and the older ones who held no rank on the Rosemary bus.

In that bus's history, there had been a running war between the boys and the girls, carried on in the past by older brothers and sisters, cousins and friends. After us, it would be fought by the younger ones who learned the rules of it from us. Sometimes a truce came about, especially if one of the boys started going with one of the girls and they sat together, holding hands or, if they were bold, kissing and petting. But mostly there was a constant effort among the hell-raising boys to make the girls lose their tempers. Seating had a lot to do with it; tougher girls, who enjoyed the battle, took the dangerous seats in back; more timid girls found safer seats toward the front. I began picking on those Rosemary girls; it was easy for me to get them upset. If one of them wore a new blouse or skirt or jacket, I would compliment her on it at length until everyone's attention fell on that girl. The same with a different lipstick or perfume. George Oglesby followed my example, and together with Herbert and Botch we succeeded in putting

Janet Littrel in tears one afternoon. I also became a hair-
puller, a bra-snapper, an ass-pincher, a trash-mouth. Those
girls had known me all through grade school and the beginning of high school as a nice boy. They lectured me, told
me to be ashamed of myself, asked me what my mother would
think of the way I was misbehaving. I told them they were
stupid. I called Molly Whisnant a bitch. George and Herbert
and Botch were on my side, slapping my shoulder, speaking
up for me. That afternoon, when the bus stopped at the
bottom of our hill to let me out, Lenore Swenson and Harriet
Weatherman held on to my belt and shirttail from behind
when I started up the aisle. Judy Statler, who was almost as
tall as I was and a good deal heavier, came back from the
front toward me. She slapped my face a couple of times.
When I had my arms up, clutching at my glasses, she punched
me in the stomach. The others let go of me, Judy let me
pass, and they pushed me up the aisle toward the door. I
could hardly breathe when I stumbled off the bus. I could
hear those girls jeering at me through the open windows when
the bus was a long way up the road from where I stood.

A Saturday night toward the end of May, the Mellowtones
played the Elks Club Spring Dance in Gantley. Patch and I
got ourselves giggling-drunk on moonshine whiskey an Elks
couple kept giving us, "to sample," they said. The woman,
with her hair in an enormous beehive, kept asking us how
we liked the stuff, we kept taking more, and her ruddy-faced
husband watched us with his eyes dancing. Gantley was in
Mercy County, near where Darcy lived; I hoped she would
come into the dance and see me drunk and acting stupid with
Patch on the bandstand.

Driving back to Madison in Dr. Kahn's station wagon, Mr.
Oliver sat in the back seat with Patch and me and chewed us

out. He said he was disappointed in both of us. He thought we'd violated the personal trust of the older members of the band as well as disregarded the standards of professional musicians. "You boys think anybody wants to hire a bunch of drunks to come in and play for them?" Patch and I said we did not. Mr. Oliver escorted us into the Madison Greyhound Bus Terminal and made us sit at a table and swill down coffee until he was certain I could drive home all right. As he left, he told us he would have a long talk with us soon to see if he thought we could be responsible enough to continue playing in the dance-band. He said he would have to discuss the matter with the other men first. On the road, all the way from Madison to Rosemary, Patch and I complained about how he had kept calling us kids and how they paid us only half of what they got even though we put in a full night's work, too. If they kept treating us as children, then how did they expect us to behave?

When I got the car into the garage and came in the house, I found my mother and father sitting up late. They weren't waiting for me, my mother said, they were just talking in the kitchen. It was three in the morning. Mother was in her bathrobe, but my father was still fully dressed. I told them I couldn't remember if I'd ever seen them awake at that time of the morning. They didn't say anything to that. They both looked serious, but they apparently didn't mean to carry on their conversation while I was there listening to them. I felt cranky anyway, from the moonshine and then the coffee and Mr. Oliver's lecture.

"What is the topic of our discussion?" I asked. I went to the stove and poured myself a cup of their coffee. Then I pulled out a chair for myself at the kitchen table and sat down with them. My mother sat looking at my father, and then she gave me a hard stare. "Reed!" she said.

"What?"

"You smell like a distillery, Son," she said.

My father didn't have anything to say to me. He looked at me over his glasses in such a way that it was clear he didn't have much use for how I was right then. He also looked like he didn't really want to have to address himself to the issue of my delinquency at that hour of the morning. I told them that Patch and I had accidentally got to drinking moonshine whiskey, that we didn't know what it was until we'd had right much of it. "You know it's clear as water," I said. My father and my grandfather liked to tell Duncan and me about the old-timey moonshiners around Rosemary and Gantley, the ones who would throw horse turds in their mash to make it ferment faster. I knew I wasn't being overwhelmingly convincing, but they both looked so worn-out that I decided they were ready to buy just about anything I tried to sell them. I said that Patch and I had stopped at the bus terminal in Madison and drunk coffee until we were certain we were sober before we drove home. My mother didn't say anything when I finished that story, just turned her eyes toward my father.

"That doesn't sound so good, boy," my father said. He made me mad the way he said it. I looked him straight in the eye. He was really no bigger than I was, I thought. His skin was pale and mottled, he was losing his hair, his breathing had a rasp in it.

"Look," I said, "I'm tired of being a goddamn boy!" and I was shouting by the time I finished saying it. My mother lifted her eyebrows and looked first at me, then at my father. "You will have to excuse me," she said. "I think it's time for me to go to bed."

"I mean it," I said as she got up from the table.

"I know you do, Son. Goodnight." She reached across the table and patted my father's shoulder. "Goodnight," she said to him. She went out, leaving my father sitting there with me across the table, under the washed-out kitchen lights. We could hear her footsteps upstairs for a while, until she got in bed.

"Like for instance," I said, startling myself with the violation of silence my voice made, "before I came in here, you and Mother were talking about something important. And then you both got all hush-hush, like the child just can't handle the adult topics, you know. How do you think that makes me feel?" I took my glasses off and polished them with a napkin my mother had left at her place.

"Oh Lord, Son," my father said. I could tell he was tired. But I was making a point. I knew I had a momentum then that I wasn't likely to have again anytime soon. I didn't let up on him.

"Well?" I said. He looked at me over his hands, which he'd been using to rub his eyes. I kept staring at him, straight on.

"Darcy," my father said. "We were talking about Darcy. We were talking about whether or not I was going to have to fire Darcy." He said it like something he'd memorized, something he'd had to memorize that he didn't like. What he said surprised me. I kept quiet for a while. But he continued looking at me. I felt like he was giving me some kind of a test; if I handled myself all right through this conversation, then maybe he would start treating me with some respect. "What is your opinion?" he finally asked.

I let a few seconds go by before I answered him. "I don't know all the facts," I said.

"Mrs. Oglesby has complained again," he said, "that Bernard cannot concentrate on his family obligations without being distracted by Darcy Webster. Mrs. Agee and Mrs. Blevins have made telephone calls to me in the past week to make accusations against Darcy Webster. They say their husbands, who have both been excellent husbands in the past, have now gone to the dogs because of Darcy Webster." He waited for me to say something.

"Those are just accusations," I said. "What about you? Have you seen her do anything wrong?" I noticed that we were both speaking in formal tones, as if this were some kind of official proceeding.

"No," my father said. "I have seen Willie Agee hanging around Darcy's desk a good part of the day, and I have directed Willie Agee to keep his butt out of there since none of his duties require him to be in her office. I have seen Jake Blevins trying to engage Darcy in conversation, but it was clear to me that Darcy did not want to talk with Jake at that time and in that place, which was at lunchtime in the hallway just outside the women's bathroom. In my opinion, it's only Slick Mallory, whose wife has made no complaint, who might have some reason to devote any of his time to thinking about Darcy Webster. One afternoon I did see Darcy hand him an envelope as he walked by her desk. I do not know what was in the envelope."

"You've really been keeping an eye on her," I told him. I felt myself getting edgy. I couldn't help it. That vision of Darcy handing an envelope to Slick Mallory bothered me— even though I wasn't sure I even knew which one of the carbide men Slick Mallory was. I didn't like my father's telling me about it, either.

"Yes," he said. "I've had to watch her because people have been accusing her. I have thought that I might have to fire her. She has been a good worker. She was a great help to me and to several of the men that afternoon of the burning accident. From my experience with her, I find it hard to believe that she is not of excellent character. The envelope she handed

Slick Mallory might have contained merely a letter he had asked her to type for him. If I am going to have to fire her, I want to be as fair about it as possible."

"You want to be in the right," I said. I could tell that got to him. I could tell I'd got him a good one with that. He'd been slumped in his chair while he talked before, but now he sat up straight.

"That's right," he said. "I want to be in the right." His glasses glittered at me, and his voice was tight, but he was holding his temper pretty well.

"I think she's kind of flirty," I said. I felt my stomach cramp. I barely had enough breath in my lungs to get out the last part of the sentence. I made my face hold still, made my eyes look directly at him.

"What?" my father said.

I shrugged. "On the bus," I said. "They talk about her. They say things."

"Who says things? What do they say?" My father's voice was up a half-tone from what it had been. I knew I had to be careful, had to hold steady.

"Just those guys," I said. "Herbert and Patch and George and T.W. They don't say much. Just they mention her name and then laugh. You know how they do it sometimes."

"No, I don't know," my father said. He was quiet for a while, and then he leaned back in his chair, folded his hands on the table in front of him. "Those are only accusations," he said. "Have you seen her do anything wrong?"

"Not really wrong," I said.

"Flirty, then," my father said. His tone was going back to normal. He was about to end the conversation, I thought.

"Yes," I said. "At a dance where I played. She came with one man, but she spent a lot of time with someone else."

"What dance was this?"

"The Soiree Club dance at the country club," I told him.
"Last month."

"Who was the man she came with?"

"Phil somebody. I don't know his last name. That new
contractor in Madison."

"And who was the man she spent a lot of time with?"

"I don't know him."

My father repeated it all to himself, as if it were a puzzle
and if he went over it carefully, the answer would come to
him. "She came with a man named Phil. She spent time
with a man you don't know."

"Yes sir."

"You saw that with your own eyes," my father said.

"Yes sir."

"And you call that flirty?"

"I don't know what else you could call it," I said.

My father was quiet for a long while. Then he said very
quietly, "She's not that kind of person. I don't believe you."
He was speaking from way down inside himself, his eyelids
half closed, as if he weren't even aware that I was sitting there
across the table from him.

"Well, don't, then," I said. I got up from the table and
went upstairs to my room. I hurried to undress, get in bed,
turn the light out, but I was too slow. He was up there right
away. I could hear his footsteps coming toward my door. He
knocked, but he didn't wait for me to tell him to come in.
He opened the door while I had my pants half off. I sat down
on the bed and tried to glare at him.

"I want you to know I'm going to fire her," he said. "I just
made up my mind."

"It's your decision," I said.

"I appreciate your helping me make it," he answered. And
closed the door.

I stayed awake a long time that night thinking about him, how he wouldn't let go his hold on me. I imagined how he would have to speak to Darcy and tell her that she was fired. I knew she would cry: I could see her, in one of her bright dresses, standing in front of his desk, with her arms down, letting her tears come down her face. I knew she would ask him to explain to her why he was firing her. And I knew that would do some damage to him. Not enough, though. I expected he would tell me about the firing, make me listen to every detail. Finally I did hit upon something I could do that might shake him loose from me. If I embarrassed him in front of the men who worked for him, that would be a terrible thing for him, I decided.

We had a sullen Sunday breakfast. I ate methodically and tried to keep a pleasant expression on my face while I forked down my scrambled eggs. My mother asked my father if it was all right for her to have the car the next day, and he told her that it was. I asked, with elaborate politeness, if I might be allowed to be the one who drove to meet him there at the carbide plant that afternoon. My mother said, "Yes, if that's all right with your father." My father said nothing. I guessed he meant it was all right.

That Monday afternoon I drove slowly to the plant, enjoying the sunlight on the trees and fields and on the river where it turned the brown water into molten silver. I knew that when I saw my father I would call out something to him, loud enough for the men around him to hear it, about Darcy. I would shout at him and ask him if he had gotten rid of her, fired her, sacked her. I might even call her a name. I hadn't made up my mind exactly what I would say, but I knew generally what it was going to be. I would trust my tongue to improvise, to give the right words.

When I drove up past the warehouses and across the railroad tracks, I saw that Darcy's car was gone from its usual place and that her place was now empty. I knew for sure then that my father had fired her. Sometime around the middle of the morning she would have come out of the gatehouse, walked to her car, and driven home. I was sure my father had talked to her before lunchtime. He never delayed doing difficult things, liked to get them out of the way as soon as possible. I decided it would be a nice touch if I parked in Darcy's spot and waited for him there, with the car pointed toward the gatehouse where he would come out. I felt exhilarated while I tried to sit still there and wait for him. I knew something important was going to happen.

One or two men began to straggle out of the gatehouse, the way some of them did, knowing they wouldn't be reprimanded or docked any pay for leaving only a few minutes early. Then the whistle blew the official four-thirty quitting time, and the men began to stream out of the gatehouse. I watched them intently, noted their dark faces, their hats, the way their shoulders curled inward toward their chests, their sweat-marked gray and khaki and dark-blue clothes, the way they carried their dinner-buckets hooked down on the ends of their fingers as if they'd as soon drop them as carry them home. I made no attempt to greet those men, though I knew many of them. My window was open as they passed by me, but I did not speak to them. I noticed one or two men nod as they walked by me, but I did not think of nodding back or raising my hand. I concentrated on the men coming out of the door of the gatehouse where they appeared in thick packs of faces. I wanted to be certain I could see my father when he first appeared, to be certain I would correctly time whatever it was that I was going to shout out at him.

After a while I became aware of how tightly my hands were gripping the steering wheel and how they felt cramped and tired. I saw that the stream of men who got off work at four-thirty had passed. Only the late three or four were coming out of the gatehouse now. Most of the cars and pickup trucks were running and pulling out in the brief swarm of traffic and swirling dust that occurred every time the shifts changed. The lightness and excitement I'd felt a few minutes earlier turned into a gloomy anger. I felt as if I were holding a heavy object in the center of my stomach, just under my breastbone. No more men came out of the gatehouse. I made myself take my hands off the steering wheel, put them in my lap. I wondered if there'd been some mistake, if my father had called home to say he'd be staying late, or maybe had taken a trip to Madison or Gantley and had not gotten back yet.

Then I decided he was doing it to me on purpose, making me wait out there like that, as if my time had no value. He was keeping his hold on me. My neck and ears began burning while I sat there, and I decided I would leave him.

I started the car, but just then I saw him come out of the gatehouse, alone, his hat pushed back in that way he wore it when he was very tired, when he'd had the worst kind of a day. His clothes drooped on him. They were gray and his face was gray, carbide-coated. The car was running. I put it into drive and began coasting toward him. I saw him look at me across the hood of the car. I edged the steering wheel over toward him a little. I headed the car directly at him, pressing the accelerator just enough to pick up a mile or two of speed. It worked. He thought I was going to hit him, and he scuttled over toward the chain-link fence, took hold of it with his hand, and raised his foot. When I was almost on him, I flicked the steering wheel away, slammed on the brakes at exactly the right moment. The car slid to a stop with the door handle right at his hand. He leaned down to look in the window at me. I could see every line in his face, could hear him breathing hard.

"Joke," I said.

He kept staring at me, bending down to see in the windc but not yet opening the door. His face was a way I'd never seen it before. It was a way I had known he was going to look at me, I had thought at one time, far out in the future.

"Joke," I said again, through my clenched teeth.

The

Wedding Storm

I'm not going to count on them," Duncan's voice in
the telephone receiver told me. He meant our parents.
Mother was standing right behind me, with her hand on my
back, waiting to speak to him.

"Duncan," I started to argue with him, but I felt my mother's hand press against me when she heard my voice take on
that tone. "What?" he said, and I said, "Here's Mother."

Duncan and Eleanor, the soft-voiced Madison girl he had
started dating that past summer, had decided to marry. Our
parents never said aloud that they didn't want Duncan to
marry, but it was that, their never saying it directly to him,
that upset him. He knew how they felt, because in our family,
signals were given. For instance, there was the prediction of
bad weather. My mother and Aunt Patricia, my grandmother
on my mother's side and Great Aunt Winnie, my grandmother on my father's side and Clara Pickett, the woman who
came once a week to do my grandmother's washing, and even

my father, too, all had it fixed firmly in their minds that it would snow and that the roads would be bad on Duncan's wedding day.

From the living room, where my father and I had resumed the chess game Duncan's call had interrupted, we could hear my mother telling him, "The weather might be . . ." She stopped, and I could imagine Duncan shouting into the pay phone at the end of his dormitory hallway, pounding the wall's painted concrete block with his open palm, *Good Lord, Mother, I'm getting married! The weather is not* . . . We heard her say, "I know, Son, I know you are, but we have to think about these things, and we're not always able to anticipate . . ." Then she stopped again, waited a long time to hear whatever it was Duncan was saying, and finally told him, "All right, Son. We'll do the best we can. Yes. Yes. Goodbye."

The phone went down in its cradle. The study was quiet. My father and I knew she was still sitting there at his desk, considering the things she and Duncan had said to each other, probably tilting back my father's desk chair, staring out the window, facing the winter night and her own reflection in the glass.

Across the chessboard, my father asked, "Is it my turn yet?" I told him no, I was still thinking. He paused, then asked, "Did Duncan say how his grades were looking this semester?"

My father was devious. He wanted me to think that he was in no hurry for me to give him the knight he had so obviously trapped, that he would like to pass the time discussing with me a current family issue. But what he actually accomplished, at some level of his knowing it, too, was to distract me from our game even more than I was already distracted by the telephone conversation in the study, and to register again, for the hundredth or so time, an opinion of Duncan and Duncan's affairs in which he—my father—would not be moved.

"No," I said, after a while, "he didn't." I moved a pawn forward and let him take the knight. "That's it," I said. "I concede the game." My father tried to catch my eye, but I wouldn't look at him. I was grateful to him for not saying aloud the words that came to both our minds, *Don't give up if you've still got a chance.*

Instead, he asked, "Is that enough for the night, Son?" I told him that it was, got up from the table, went to the window to try to see out past the lighted reflections of our living room and of my own face. I listened to him put the chess pieces back into the old cigar box where he kept them.

I had missed Duncan in that house. His second year in Charlottesville, he had made terrible grades, lost his scholarship, got himself suspended, and had to go to summer school to be readmitted. Through this past fall, though, his letters home had indicated he was doing better, thanks to Eleanor's interest and encouragement. He said he wished he could show us the beautifully written letters she sent to him.

"Don't forget," my mother called from the study, "you have to pack tonight."

"Yes ma'am," I said.

"I put out some extra underwear and socks and a shirt for you," she informed me, "in case the weather goes bad and you have to stay over there."

Next morning I took my father to work at the carbide plant and then drove the car the twenty miles to my high school in Madison. I was a senior, and no one thought it was anything special for a senior, even one from Rosemary, to be bringing his parents' car to school. But with my suitcase packed with several days' worth of clothes in the trunk, with my best suit hanging up in the back seat, with my brother coming in on the *Tennessean* that afternoon, I was too excited to give much thought to classes. At lunchtime, standing with Annie beside her opened locker, I slipped my hand under her sweater and tickled the bare skin over her ribs. She ducked away from me, asking, so loudly that heads in the hallway turned toward us, "Reed, what's the matter with you?" But her voice was engaging, and her eyes looked me up and down.

After school, without much time, I drove Annie home, followed her into the kitchen, pressed her back against the refrigerator, and pushed against her while we kissed. When Mrs. Moore came downstairs we were sitting across from each other at the kitchen table, discussing Mrs. Yerkes, who had recently given Annie a C. "Ann, your face is red," her mother said first thing.

"Oh," said Annie, touching her cheeks with her fingertips.

Mrs. Moore turned her eyes, which were kind but examining nevertheless, on me. "Will you stay for supper, Reed?" she asked.

"No ma'am," I told her. "I have to meet my brother at the train station." I craned my neck to look at the clock behind me. "In another couple of minutes," I said, hoping Mrs. Moore would go back upstairs.

The blackboard outside the station indicated that the *Tennessean* would arrive forty-five minutes late, and I considered driving back up to Annie's house. But I remembered that on Fridays her father left work early to spend time at home with his family and that, furthermore, I had not enjoyed those afternoons when he and Annie and I sat in the Moores' living room struggling with a conversation. I waited at the train station, first sitting on one of the huge old benches of polished, blond wood and then later going outside to pace the station platform. The day turned cold before the *Tennessean* finally pulled in. Except for the stationmaster and his helper, I was the only person there to meet the train.

"Reed, my boy," Duncan said, sticking out his hand. I

took it, and we commenced the old gripping contest, squeezing until one or the other of us gave it up, grimacing and snorting, while the conductor watched us with half a smile on his face.

"I give up," I called out, and Duncan let me go. Although Duncan was uncoordinated and unathletic, he was larger than even my father, and very strong. I was almost always the one who had to stop the gripping contest. Another of our games was the one where Duncan stuck out his stomach and demanded that I punch him there, at approximately his belt level, but he did not invite me to play that one. "I want to use the telephone," he said. I took his bag from him before he went indoors.

I expected to have to wait in the car a long while, but he came back out of the station almost immediately. I watched him walking, looking once up at the sky, blowing into his hands. "Can you take me up to Eleanor's house?" he asked before he even got the door closed. "She says I can see her now, if we hurry." He blew in his hands again and rubbed them together. "Don't look at me like that, you dolt," he said. "You can wait for me outside. I'll only be a couple of minutes."

The Stinnets' house was down at the far end of Madison, down a street on which there were only a few houses, then up a dirt lane that wound around several sharp corners. It sat alone at the top of a hill overlooking the town. Eleanor was on the front porch in the cold, waiting for my brother. Duncan swung out of the car just as I got it stopped, and they embraced with me there as their witness. I should have been embarrassed, but I wasn't; I watched them with interest. When they turned to go indoors, Eleanor gave me a wave and a smile. I kept the car and the heater and the radio turned on while I waited in the late-afternoon light.

Eleanor Stinnet always seemed to me to be looking up at

Duncan, and Duncan to be looking down at Eleanor, each of them gently regarding the other. Around her, Duncan became more considerate and quieter than I could have imagined his being before he met her. Her face was round, her hair and eyes dark, and almost always her expression was one of powerful kindness. I had noticed that I, too, spoke more carefully and in softer tones when I was talking with Eleanor.

They came out of the house together, Eleanor circling around the car to speak to me. "Hello, Reed," she said, and we shook hands through the open window. The wind made her shiver, and she rubbed her arms with her hands. "Do you think it'll snow?" she asked. "Not a chance," I told her.

They stood away from the car, talking very quietly. The light had gone so dim that they both seemed to have been swallowed by Duncan's dark overcoat. Then Duncan climbed into the car, and Eleanor went up onto her porch; they did not say goodbye or goodnight, but they continued looking at each other. "Such sweet sorrow," I said under my breath while I was turning the car around.

"Shut your mouth, Spider Nose," Duncan said. "I want food. I want bowls and plates and platters of food."

He ordered T-bone steaks for both of us at the Hampton Grill, where our family sometimes used to eat Sunday dinner after church at St. Paul's. He drank three large glasses of milk, and he ordered seconds on the blueberry pie with ice cream. When I brought out my billfold to pay my share of the check, he told me to put my money away. "When did you strike it rich?" I asked him.

"I've got a job," he whispered across the table, grinning and plucking ten-dollar bills out of his billfold. It went unspoken between us that our mother and father would strongly disapprove of his taking time away from his studies to hold a job. "It's only twenty hours a week," he told me. "Don't worry. I'm passing everything this semester."

When we went outside, the wind hit us hard, and the sidewalks were almost empty. Duncan squinted up one way and then down the other, but he didn't seem to know what he wanted to do. "Mother said we were to check into the hotel before it got too late," I told him.

"I don't feel like doing that now," he said. "Let's walk down this way a couple of blocks." We put our hands in our pockets, hunched our shoulders into the wind, and headed down Main Street. Madison wasn't really our town; it was simply where we'd both gone to high school. I thought I was feeling the same way as Duncan then, pleasantly familiar with that street and those stores and the smells in the air, but still not quite at ease.

We walked all the way up past the state liquor store, the Gulf station, and the Lutheran church. We were passing the large old houses on upper Main Street then, and though he said nothing, I thought Duncan must have meant to walk all the way down to Eleanor's house. "Duncan, I'm going back," I told him.

He looked wildly at me for a moment, but then he said, "All right, let's cross over to the other side of the street." We did that, still walking in silence, Duncan staring straight up ahead of himself, as if he were eager to get to some extraordinary place. "Walked all the way to the top of Afton Mountain one night," he said just as we reached the car.

"How come?"

"Thinking about something, I guess. Can't remember exactly. Just never did come to a place where I wanted to turn around."

I started the car and pulled it over into the hotel parking lot, which was just across the street from the Hampton Grill. Duncan sat hunched forward in the seat, his hands folded in his lap, looking as if his mind were a hundred miles away. "It's the professors who are supposed to be absent-minded," I told him.

"Yeah," he said, and he turned toward me. "Maybe that's my trouble down there." For a moment he looked so serious and forlorn that I felt like apologizing to him. Even though we were out of the wind then, it was still very cold in the car; I felt myself starting to shiver.

"Come on," I told him. "Let's go check into this place."

Our mother had reserved rooms there at the James Madison Hotel because, she said, in case of bad weather she wanted to be certain that at least the groom and the best man were able to get to the wedding. Duncan wandered around the empty lobby while I checked in with elegant, white-haired Mr. Bill Smith. Mr. Bill Smith had been the mayor of Madison for years, but then he finally lost an election and fell on hard times. People said he came to be the night desk clerk at the hotel because he loved the town's Class C baseball team so much; the baseball players were quartered there in the summer. But now, in January, almost no one stayed in the hotel. Mr. Bill Smith's elaborate manners and immaculate suit, shirt, tie, and polished shoes seemed to exist for no good purpose. He rang the desk bell, and an ancient black man, who'd been leaning against the desk a few feet away from me, picked up our suitcases, carried them to the elevator, and held the door open for Duncan and me.

Inside my room, across the hall from Duncan's, I walked around the bed, opened the curtains, and peeked through the Venetian blinds. My view was of the hotel parking lot, Red Carter's Esso station, and the side of the Madison County National Bank. I sat in the chair for a moment before getting up to check inside each of the drawers of the small bureau. Then I went into the bathroom and stared at myself for a

while in the mirror. I decided that Duncan probably intended
to stay in his room to read or to go to sleep early. I sat on
the bed reading the instructions on the telephone, trying
to figure out how to call Annie. There was a soft knock at
the door.

"Come in," I said, but then when the door remained shut
in spite of the handle clicking and turning, I went to open
it. Duncan came in with a full bottle of Cutty Sark Scotch.
"Bachelor party," he said with a droll look on his face.

When I dialed Room Service, there was no change in the
steady buzzing sound of the phone. After a while Mr. Bill
Smith's voice came on the line, "Yes sir, Mr. Bryant, what
can I do for you?" When I asked him for ice and a couple
of glasses, there was a long pause, but then he said, "Yes sir,
ice and two glasses, coming up right away." Twenty minutes
later, the ancient black man brought a tray to my door. The
ice bucket was small, and anyway it was only about half full
of cubes that looked as if they'd been taken from someone's
refrigerator at home.

"Want some water in yours?" I asked Duncan, heading for
the bathroom.

"Nope. I take mine on the rocks." He poured whisky almost
to the top of his glass, as if it were water.

"You sure you know what you're doing?" I asked him.

"Look, Pinhead," he said. "Where do you think I go to
school?" He sat in the chair, propped his feet on the radiator,
held the glass to his mouth with both hands, and made slurping noises.

I went for my water, came back, and fixed myself a comfortable backrest with pillows against the headboard of the
bed. "You were a very clean-cut fellow all through high school,"
I informed him.

"Hah! That's all you know. Maybe you don't know much."

"Yes," I said. "That's right. Maybe I don't."

We were quiet for a while, sipping our drinks. Duncan stood up, adjusted the Venetian blinds, and stared out the window with his back turned to me. "So what do you think?" he asked. "Will they be there or not?"

He was still wearing the checked sportcoat Mother had gotten him in Roanoke before he went to Charlottesville that first time. There was a spot of gray hair on the back of his head—a birthmark, my grandmother called it; I had noticed it a thousand times before. But with his back turned to me, in the bad light of the hotel room, he looked unfamiliar to me. "Do you remember when you used to bribe me to tickle your back for you?" I asked him. I felt foolish for asking it because it brought up that old time when we were little and slept in the same bed, when Duncan loved to have his pale, mole-covered back tickled until he fell asleep.

"Answer my question, Reed. Will they be there?" Duncan faced me, and I could see his eyes were narrowed, he really was angry. But then his face softened, one side of his mouth turned up into a grin, and he was the familiar Duncan. "Do you know what is maddening about our family, Egg Face?" He rattled the ice cubes in his glass as he went over to the bottle on the table.

"I can't imagine."

"Evasive," he said. "Every one of them. Ask somebody in our family a direct question; what do you get? A comment on the weather. A bit of nostalgia, a childhood memory." He turned and looked down at me.

"Like for instance," I said, "if you were to ask somebody in our family a direct question like did they think you were drinking your whisky too fast, you'd be likely to get an evasive answer like *yes*."

"That's not what I mean," he said, going back to his chair, waving his hand toward the bottle. "Plenty there. Help yourself." He paused, looking up at the ceiling, his mock-meditative posture. "Like for instance," he said, "you could walk into the study at home and ask our father if he thought you ought to remain in engineering school or take a semester off to work for Schockey Construction. Do you know what answer you'd be likely to get?"

"I didn't think you'd ever asked such a question," I told him. I got up to fill my glass with ice and whisky; I went to the bathroom for water. When I came back into the room, Duncan had already started saying his answer.

". . . telling you about Granddad and his faith in books, how Granddad took all those correspondence courses and taught himself metallurgy and surveying and calculus and how he —our father—got sick and couldn't finish . . ."

"Translate it," I said, and he rolled his eyes at me. "That's why you have so much trouble with them," I told him. "You don't translate."

"Like for instance," he went on, giving me to understand that he was not yet ready to address himself to my point, "you could walk into the kitchen and ask our mother, point-blank ask her, mind you, if you should get married, if she thinks you should get married or not." He paused for effect, but when I started to say something he went on. "For an answer you will get an Ode to Our Back Yard, a description of the forsythia, the lilacs, how much her daffodils and irises have meant to her, the beauties of our morning-glories and nasturtiums and zinnias and whatever else those things are she plants out there."

He stopped, and we both knew I was free to speak then. "Simple matter of converting language into meaning," I said in as condescending a voice as I could come up with.

"Please translate then, oh most brilliant Peacock Brain. I'm listening."

"Dad wishes he'd finished at Emory and Henry. Mother

thinks having your own house is important."

Duncan drained his glass, slumped down in the chair, tucked his chin into his chest, and looked at me through slitted eyelids. "Enlightenment at last," he said. "You've a wisdom far beyond your years, Reed, my boy. I'd say your intellectual development must be at least up to that of a six-year-old by now."

"See if I translate anything else for you," I said. I finished my drink, and we both got up at the same time to refill our glasses. "Do you think it's worth calling downstairs for more ice?" I asked him.

Duncan put his glass on the table and laid his big hands on my neck, pretending to choke me. "Do you think they'll be here tomorrow?" he whispered in my ear.

"I expect ice isn't really necessary this far along into the night," I said and dipped my fingers into the water at the bottom of the bucket and flipped a spray into Duncan's face. He loosened his grip, and I ducked away from him.

"Murky water," he said, coming toward me, putting on his monster-face, hunching his shoulders, rolling his arms out from his body.

"What's that?" I said, backing around to the head of the bed.

"In . . . this . . . family . . . you . . . must . . . swim . . . for . . . yourself," he said, coming on, making a terrible face.

"You want a lifeguard out there with you?" I asked. I grabbed the top pillow and swung at him.

"Exactly, Ferret Face," he said. He lunged after me, but I managed to put a foot on the bed and get almost across it before I felt his hands catching my shirt, pulling me back.

"You'll rip it," I told him, but he kept pulling me back.

"Clothes are nothing," he said. "Only the truth matters." I struggled, but it was not much trouble for him to put me in a full nelson, the same hold he had used on me since he was fourteen and learned it from watching television. "Now," he said, pressing my head down into my chest, "do you think they will be there tomorrow?"

"Yes," I said. "They'll be there."

"Thank you," Duncan said and let me go. We got up from the bed and straightened our clothes. "Would you like another drink, little brother?" We were both out of breath.

"Yes, I would. Thanks," I said. "I have to call Annie."

"Go right ahead," he said. "By all means, call the lovely Miss Moore." I could tell that he meant to stay right there in the room with me.

While I was dialing Annie's number and while he was fixing us both new drinks, I said, "Actually, Duncan, you just want people to give you the answers you want to hear."

He turned to look at me. "How unusual of me," he said.

Mr. Bill Smith's voice came on the line, "Yes, Mr. Bryant, what can I do for you?" I covered the receiver and told Duncan, "Apparently no matter what number you dial on this thing, you get Mr. Bill Smith."

"Makes perfect sense," he said, heading for the bathroom to put water in my drink.

Annie answered as if she'd been sitting beside the phone waiting for it to ring. "Reed, where *are* you?" she asked. I couldn't tell if her voice was signaling anger or relief.

"Having a bachelor party."

"I thought you were going to call earlier."

"Tried to," I told her. "Couldn't get through." Duncan brought me my glass and went to stand at the window again. He poked through the blinds with his fingers and then, with considerable clatter, raised them as far up as they would go.

"How many people are there?" Annie asked.

"Can hardly count 'em," I said. "The Bryant brothers are

here. Then there's a Mr. D. Bryant and a Mr. R. Bryant, and there are those Bryant boys from over at Rosemary. And of course Duncan and I are here."

"Fool," Duncan said into the windowpane just loud enough for me to hear him.

"You sound weird," Annie said. I could tell she had something she was holding back, something she wanted me to know.

"What's up, Annie?"

She wouldn't answer for a while. Then she said, "I'm here by myself, Reed," in a tiny, sad voice. I could see her pouting into the phone receiver, probably sitting there in the hallway at the Moores', twirling her hair with her fingers.

"Chance we've been waiting for," I said.

"Oh, yes, Reed," Annie's voice came all in a rush then, "I had to lie to them so they'd let me stay here, told them I had the cramps and just couldn't stand the idea of that long drive down to Grandmama's, told them I had a report due for Mrs. Lancaster on Monday. I was sure you would call, and I could fix dinner for you, and I wouldn't feel bad about it with you here."

"Annie," I said, but I didn't have anything to tell her.

"I feel terrible now."

Duncan had come away from the window and was standing over me, looking down his nose at me, obviously wanting me to get off the phone. I couldn't think what to say to Annie with him spooking me like that.

"Reed?" she said. I grunted into the phone to signal that I was still there. She went on, "Can you come over now?"

I thought a long while about it. Duncan began to make monster-faces at me. "I guess I better stay here and keep an eye on Duncan," I told her. "He's in bad shape."

"Oh, Reed," Annie said.

Duncan was doing a silent ape-dance then, and it was hard not to laugh at him. "Mother told me to watch after him."

Annie said nothing.

"I'll come by tomorrow, Annie," I told her. "After I put them on the train."

"Doesn't your brother have a car?" Annie asked. I knew she was looking for something hateful to say. I wanted to stop the conversation before we ended up in another one of our arguments.

"Trains are significant in our family. My grandfather was a fireman. See you tomorrow, Honey." I hung up, cringing to myself at how disgustingly false I sounded whenever I tried to use a word like *Honey* with Annie.

"Come on," Duncan said, yanking at my shoulder.

"What?"

"Get your coat." He was out the door, across the hall, working the key to get into his own room. "Hurry up," he said.

In the hallway, I started to push the button for the elevator, but Duncan was already heading for the door to the steps. We clattered down three flights in the boxlike stairwell. When we crossed the lobby, Mr. Bill Smith rose and stood grandly behind the desk, spoke to us—"Good evening, gentlemen" —as if recognizing two such distinguished ones as Duncan and me in a milling crowd of hotel guests. Our footsteps rang on the marble floor of the empty lobby.

Outside it was snowing terrifically.

Duncan and I stood on the white-columned verandah, where some summer evenings boys our age, baseball players, lined up to sit in rocking chairs and whistle at passing Madison girls. We watched that white stuff come down as if someone were shoveling it out of a barn loft.

It was after midnight. The stoplights up and down the street had switched to blinking on yellow. Only a few cars were parked anywhere within sight. Duncan and I, without saying anything, walked down the steps onto the softly covered sidewalks. Ours were the only footprints we could see in the new snow.

When we turned down Main Street, I caught a glimpse of Mr. Bill Smith standing at the door of the hotel, his hands behind his back, watching us. He lifted a hand, and Duncan gave him a salute.

"Well, Vladimir," Duncan said, "Will we ever see St. Petersburg again?"

"Not in our time, Boris," I told him.

Already the snow was more than an inch thick. In the dark places of the sidewalk it was a deep blue with brilliant sparkles on its surface. At each store it took the coloring of the window-lights and the neon signs. Duncan and I marched crisply past the Soda Shop, Greenwald's, Leggett's, the old Madison Theatre, Piggly-Wiggly, Western Auto, Honest to Pete's, the Farmers and Merchants Bank.

"I'm getting cold, Duncan," I shouted at him. He had taken on that dreamy forward-staring look of his.

"Onward, Vladimir," he shouted. "Don't give up yet!"

We passed on to upper Main Street and the big houses, the lawns and trees of which were now freshly whitened. I felt something like homesickness working on me when I looked at the dark houses.

"I'm going back now, Duncan," I said. He turned, and we both crossed Main Street, heading back down toward the Lutheran church, the Gulf station, the liquor store. When we passed under the streetlight, Duncan ducked his head away from me.

"Are you all right?" I asked him.

"Ah, Vladimir," he said, "how kind of you to ask after the Colonel's health."

In the hotel lobby Mr. Bill Smith stood by the elevator, waiting for us. "Gentlemen," he said and held the door open for us, "never walk when you can ride. Just push the button for your floor, and when it stops, slide both doors open. Goodnight, gentlemen."

"Polite old geezer for an embezzler," Duncan said while we were heading up to the third floor.

"Embezzler?" I was leaning hard against the side of the elevator.

"Sure, that's what he did. Why do you think he's night clerk at this joint?"

"I feel pretty bad, Duncan," I told him when he opened the elevator doors. "Maybe we should have walked up."

"Nonsense," he said. "The Colonel never walks."

We each turned to our doors, but mine was too far away, and I was about to fall. "Oh Jesus, Duncan," I said.

He opened my door for me and helped me to the bathroom. I threw up for a long time. Finally I flushed it away, got up from the floor, and washed my face at the sink. When I came back into the room, Duncan was standing at the window, looking out at the snow.

"You all right now?" he asked.

"Doesn't that stuff make you sick?" I asked him.

"I guess not," he said. "Tonight's the first time I ever drank any of it." He stood at the door and waited until I was undressed and in bed. Then he switched off the light and went out.

The phone woke me. My father was speaking from downstairs at his desk, my mother from upstairs at the phone on her bedside table. They could not come to the wedding because of the bad weather and the roads.

"I told him you'd be here." I almost shouted into the receiver.

"We've already spoken with your brother," my mother said.

"He understands perfectly. He knows we love him. And Eleanor, too," she said.

"I think you should at least try."

"Not in your grandmother's car are we going to try it," my father said. "Reed, we didn't ask for this storm. We don't like it any better than you do."

"I think you *do* like it," I said, and then I was shouting. "I think it's exactly what you wanted!" I said, and I put down the receiver.

At breakfast, across the street at Hampton's Grill, I picked at my food, stared out the window at shopkeepers and clerks clearing snow from the sidewalks in front of their stores. Duncan ate a bowl of cereal, two eggs with ham, fried potatoes, juice, milk, and coffee. He handed me the tiny wedding band for Eleanor's finger and said, "Lose it, Long Face, and you die."

We walked back to the hotel, got dressed for the wedding, packed our suitcases. Duncan came to my room to wait for me. He said that Eleanor's parents had agreed not to attend the wedding.

"Balance?" I asked, and Duncan nodded.

This time, when we stepped outside, the sun had come out strongly, and traffic on Main Street was picking up. We squinted our eyes in what seemed like too much light everywhere. I drove the car with our suitcases in it up to St. Paul's, but Duncan walked and beat me there.

We met Mr. Norcross, already in his robes, in the vestibule and stood talking with him until Eleanor and her sister and her brother arrived. Duncan and Eleanor gave each other a hug and a kiss. Then we listened while Mr. Norcross explained to us how the wedding would be.

Five of us walked into the empty church, Mr. Norcross in front, Duncan and Eleanor behind him, then Eleanor's sister, the maid of honor, and I, the best man. One light came down from high over the altar. Three candles burned on either side of a gold cross. Our steps made no noise on the soft carpet of the aisle. Colors of light beaming in through the stained-glass windows washed over us as we walked. At the altar steps, Mr. Norcross turned. We lined up in front of him, Duncan holding himself very straight, he and Eleanor looking steadily at each other.

My heart jumped when Duncan looked at me to hand him the ring for Eleanor. I looked in the wrong pocket and saw Duncan beginning to smile at me, could almost hear him saying, *Stupid, stupid* Vladimir. When I found it and handed it to him, I noticed that sweat had come on his forehead.

Then the wedding was done, and Eleanor's brother came into the church to take pictures of us. While he was showing us where to stand, he laughed and said that he had been able to hear almost none of the ceremony from the vestibule where he had waited, except when Duncan spoke his words. "I'll bet they heard you all the way over in Rosemary, Duncan," he said and laughed.

I drove Duncan and Eleanor to the wedding party at her brother's house. He was a farmer, and he had spent most of the morning on his tractor, clearing out the long driveway to his house. Driving out of Madison to his place, I listened to Duncan and Eleanor *ooh* and *ah* over the landscapes the snow had made beautiful. I was astonished at how banal my brother became in the presence of his new bride.

Eleanor's cousins were, except for the oldest and the young-est, all little girls, and they arranged themselves so as to be able to stare at the bride and groom at all times. Most of us gathered in the dining room, where there was an old Franklin stove and a table with enough food on it to feed everybody in the house for another week. "We didn't know how many would come," Eleanor's sister-in-law explained to me.

I was handed a plate heaped with ham, turkey, gravy, dressing, potatoes, vegetables, sauces, pickles, and olives. I set it on a small table near the window, and from time to time I took a bite. I was asked by members of Eleanor's family if I was all right, if they could get me anything, if there was anything else I would like. I took a small piece of the wedding cake after the bride and groom had cut it and tasted it. Duncan and Eleanor spent most of their time talking quietly with Eleanor's parents, who were, in my opinion, old enough to be her grandparents. "She was the baby," the maid of honor told me. "They'll miss her. She came late in their lives."

"She's beautiful," was all I could think to say about my new sister-in-law. And once when I was left standing alone with her and wanted to say something meaningful to her, I found I was given the same words again, "You were beautiful this morning, Eleanor." I felt I had said something foolish and wrong, but Eleanor put her arm around my shoulder, kissed me, smiled at me a long moment.

In spite of the cold, all of Eleanor's family, even old Mr. and Mrs. Stinnet, bundled in their coats, came out on the front porch to see the couple off. When we were far enough away from the rice-throwing cousins, Duncan and Eleanor and I rolled down our windows to wave at them while we headed out the long driveway. In several places, where the snow had drifted, I could see that Eleanor's brother had had to scrape and re-scrape his road to clear it for us. I could imagine him out there just at daylight, sitting on his tractor with his cheeks red and his nose running. I started to say something about it to Eleanor, but she and Duncan were whispering to each other. I held my silence all the way to the train station.

The *Washingtonian*, according to the schedule posted outside the station, had been delayed three hours. "Oh my God," I said aloud to Duncan and Eleanor, but they were amused at how upset I was.

"It'll get here, my boy. It'll get here," Duncan said. He snapped his fingers and directed me to carry the suitcases indoors. The waiting room was empty. Duncan and Eleanor stood at the ticket window joking with the stationmaster. Then they settled down on one of the benches with their luggage all around them. I began pacing, dreading the long wait. Eleanor laughed aloud and called over to me, "Reed, we almost forgot about you."

Duncan came over and stuck out his hand, but I wouldn't take it. "I'll wait here with you," I said. "I'll see you off."

"Don't be foolish, Vladimir," he said. "They will be waiting for you in St. Petersburg." He kept his hand held toward me, and finally I took it. "The Colonel is grateful to you," he said.

Eleanor stood with us then. She and I kissed each other's cheeks. I promised to visit them when they'd fixed up their apartment. At the door I exchanged salutes with Duncan. From outside, I looked in the station window and saw them sitting on the bench again, smiling as if they meant to settle down and begin their married lives right in that place.

I drove to the Greyhound Bus Terminal, parked, from my suitcase dug out my shaving kit and a clean shirt, and went into the men's room. I took off my jacket, shirt, and tie, and hung them up; I washed my face and neck and arms. I shaved for the second time that day, even though I didn't really need to. Then I combed my hair, slapped lotion on my face, and put on my fresh shirt. When I had my jacket on again, I tried standing both close to and far away from the mirror, but I was not satisfied with how I looked.

Annie was in her bathrobe when she opened the door. She had been crying, and she looked terrible. I passed into the Moores' house with neither of us saying a word. She closed the door and stood with her back against it. "I have cramps," she said. A strand of light-brown hair fell down almost into her eyes, but she didn't brush it back.

I came to her and embraced her, but I might as well have put my arms around a bathrobe on one of the mannequins in Leggett's store window. She kept her hands in her pockets, her only acknowledgment of me being to lean her head slightly forward to rest it on my shoulder. "Why didn't you come last night?" she said into the cloth of my suit jacket.

"Duncan was depending on me," I told her, and immediately I could hear Duncan's voice mocking me, *Ah, Vladimir, you moron, you imbecile.*

Annie moved away from me and walked toward the kitchen. I followed her. On the table in there were a cup of tea half gone, a pile of magazines, a box of stationery, and a stack of her schoolbooks. She sat down without offering me anything, and so I fixed myself a cup of instant coffee. I sat down across from her and told her about the wedding.

Around four o'clock the Moores' station wagon pulled into the driveway. Annie's mother and father came into the house the back way, through the kitchen where we were sitting. I got up to shake hands with Mr. Moore. "I'm glad you're back," Annie said to them. "Reed thinks he may have to spend the night because of the slick roads. I feel horrible. I'm going to bed." Annie left the kitchen, keeping her hands stuck down in her bathrobe pockets, not saying goodbye, not looking at me once.

"You're welcome to spend the night, Reed," Mrs. Moore told me, her kind eyes searching my face in that way she had of making me think she knew everything Annie and I had ever done or talked about doing. "But the roads are fine. We were over in your end of the county just a while ago, and we had no trouble at all."

I thanked her and told her that my information must have been incorrect but I was glad to hear the roads had been cleared. She and Mr. Moore walked me through the living room. Just as I stepped off their front porch, she asked me how the wedding had gone.

"It was beautiful," I told her. *Expanding your vocabulary, Vladimir?*

"I'm sure it was," Mrs. Moore said. We waved, and she stepped back inside.

I felt lightheaded as I drove out of Madison. The late-afternoon sun gave the snow-covered lawns and houses of the town a pale-orange glow. When I passed the High Hat Drive-In at the very edge of town, that parking lot had been scraped down to the bare cinders, and it was beginning to fill with cars.

I drove straight down Route 18 to Fort Ellis, turned off on Route 31 for a couple of miles, then took a final turn onto narrow, winding Route 74, which would take me all the way to Rosemary. Even 74 had been cleared of snow; it was dry, as if there'd been no bad weather at all. *Comrade, they'll be sitting in the study, waiting for you. They'll have a warm supper ready to give you, and they'll be delighted to see you. They'll want you to tell them about the wedding.*

This was the road I had known, it seemed to me, almost before I was born. Every road sign, every field, every house, every patch of scrub cedars or white pines was familiar to me. The sun's orange color deepened, and the light falling on the snow turned it such gorgeous shades of scarlet and pink and orange that my eyes flinched away from the brightness and sought out shadow. *They'll know you have reason to be angry at them, Vladimir. They'll know you'll be tempted to say things that will damage them.*

Cars I passed were beginning to switch from parking lights to headlights. When I made the last curve and came around that bend, the whole town of Rosemary lay tucked in its valley before me, the soft evening sky shining just enough for me to be able to make out shapes of houses, snow-covered roofs. I felt giddy, nervous, as if my stomach were pressing up into my chest. I wanted—stupidly, I knew—to stop the car, get out, and look into the lighted windows, the warm rooms.

I drove slowly along the highway around the edge of Rosemary's valley. When I came to where the road passed below my own house, I bent down in the seat to try to see up the hill and catch a glimpse of its light. I thought I saw it, but then I wasn't sure. When I was making the sharp turns that took me toward our driveway, I began to feel what I had always imagined people felt when they were about to faint. My heart hammered. I went on into the driveway, which had been plowed clear then, and I made myself keep going until I had rounded two of its corners and had taken the car up to the top of the ridge where I could again see the valley and the town. There I stopped, turned off the car, turned out the lights, and lay down in the front seat to wait out whatever thing it was that was working on me.

Poor Vladimir. I'm beginning to worry about your health, dear fellow. You know, the Colonel enjoys a vigorous metabolism and cannot tolerate subordinates who are forever vomiting in hotels and lying down in car seats. Please get up, go home, and await further instructions. The Colonel will be in touch.

I began to shiver after a while, in there with no heater on. I sat up, started the car, turned on the lights, and let the thing coast down the hill to our house. When I came out of the garage with my suitcase, I saw my parents silhouetted, waiting for me outside with the porch light behind them. I walked on the cleared path through the snow. My mother put her arms around me, and my father shook my hand, as if I were the one who'd gotten married instead of Duncan. "How were the roads?" my father asked as we were going indoors.

"They were beautiful," I told him.

◆ ◆ ◆ ◆ ◆ ◆ ◆ ◆ ◆ ◆ ◆ ◆ ◆ ◆ ◆

Save One

for Mainz

I had a girlfriend who wasn't beautiful. Six months out of Fort Benning, Georgia, and five months overseas, there I was at a *Fasching* party, in a crowd of shouting Germans. She was standing in front of me asking me to dance with her. She wore a white shift and dark-blue tights. She had on a carnival mask, too, but even so, I could see she was too long in the jaw. She was thin in the waist and hips, and she was big-breasted. She carried herself in a prideful way that I liked. She said her name was Hilda and she worked for a travel agency. She said I resembled another American she'd known. "Are you a loony son of a bitch?" she asked me. "Are you a crazy bastard?"

I told her, yes, that was me, all right. She said that the other American she'd known had been Airborne Infantry and that he had been violent and reckless. She asked me if I was Airborne, and I nodded my head yes. "Infantry?" she asked, and I told her no, my branch was Personnel. "What did you say?" she said. I had to shout above the music and the noise, "Personnel!"

We danced in that huge beer-hall with a wooden floor that trembled with the weight of all of us. The Germans were singing drunk, "Once Along the Rhine," arm in arm, swaying with each other around the big tables. Old men with their mouths stretched open to sing to the rafters were squeezing up young girls whose breasts were about to burst from dirndls, and red-faced women with bosoms like cheese-wheels were draping thick arms over the shoulders of young men my age. I was indeed among foreigners, but I swayed and hummed right along with them, adding my voice to that deep, sweet music, holding onto Hilda and remembering old times beside the big river. I was deeply moved, my eyes tearing up, and I decided that World War II had been entirely logical if you thought about it.

The band played a polka, and I couldn't dance the polka, but Hilda insisted, pouted her lips and clucked her tongue at me. I was drunk and didn't give a damn if I looked like a fool. I took her hand, I took her waist and began to fling my feet around the floor. It worked. I let the spirit of the polka enter me. I could feel muscles moving in Hilda's hips, and her hand on my hand, her hand on my shoulder, told me where to direct our bodies. The floor vibrated beneath us. I became lightheaded, giddy. When the music stopped, we stood back from each other and laughed and laughed. Hilda clasped her hands between her knees and cackled. I took her mask off then. She looked as I had expected she would, too much jaw and a nose that was too small for the rest of her face. She wasn't beautiful, or even pretty, but she wasn't homely either.

And she had an elegant smile. She didn't use it a lot, but when she did, her features ordered themselves into exactly the right perspective. She was blond and kept her hair cut short, so that it flicked around her face when she moved her head. Her underwear was flowered, or striped, or polka-dotted, or lacy and delicate. She spent too much on it, and so she insisted I notice it before one or the other of us took it off. If I didn't say anything, then she modeled it for me, and I had to come up with a sentence that pleased her before she stopped the posing. "You look charming in that, Hilda" was the sentence that worked best with her. She liked the word *charming* and would say it, rolling the *r* down in her throat like something good she was eating.

Sometimes she was complimentary and encouraging to me, too. "Reed, you know, you're not a bad lover," she said.

She lay and talked up toward the ceiling, running one hand over my chest and arms and neck and stomach, as if she were trying to learn my body, memorize it. Then I would see her touching herself, running thumb and finger down her rib cage, pushing at her breasts with the tips of her fingers, testing her stomach muscles. I liked to hear her talk when she was like that, even though I knew she was mostly waiting for me, waiting to see if I wanted more of her. She told me about her German boyfriend. His name was Manfred. He was a carpenter. She figured she would marry Manfred in a couple of years. It was understood, she said. From her tone, I couldn't tell if it was an understanding that appealed to her. Hilda was very objective about Manfred. She said he treated her the way German men treat German women, without much consideration. She said she preferred my company because I was nice to her. I thought about that and decided that she was right, I *was* nice to her. Also, she said, I had the apartment where we could go. She called my two rooms with a bath between them an apartment. Manfred had a good car but no place to go. It was humiliating, Hilda said, in the back seat, the business of hanging one leg over the front seat and propping the other one up in the back window. She demonstrated the contorted position for me. She said I was a better lover than Manfred. I said I thought she was probably right.

"But you're just a boy," she said. "You're a boy, and you don't yet know what you like," she said. Then she started tickling me.

I knew I had a baby face. It was probably why I hadn't been commissioned in Infantry, as I'd wanted to be. But I was one shaped-up soldier in my uniform, no doubt about that; I was Airborne all the way. I had my fatigue pants pegged all the way up to my crotch. I had my fatigue shirts taken in to fit skin-tight at my waist and chest and in the arms and shoulders. I'd soaked all those uniforms in hot water with strong bleach in it. I always asked for double starch when I sent my stuff to the laundry. I could soldier with the best of them.

My job was not demanding. I had a lot of time to myself, and Hilda was good company for me, even if she was too straightforward for her own good, even if she embarrassed me sometimes. She'd get up from bed and go wash herself unabashedly. She'd stand at the sink and use my washcloth, bending her knees outward like a ballet dancer and talking to me all the while. She chattered at me while she sat on the john, and once, when I tried to close the door on her, she accused me of rudeness. I decided that in some ways she was abnormal. She wouldn't have anything to do with my trying to learn German. She laughed at me, or else she said, very condescendingly, "Speak English, please."

She told me her mother watched her at home for signs that she might be seeing Americans. Her mother suspected her, and it made her mother furious. Once her mother called her names. Hilda shouted out the names in German and pushed her hair down over her eyes, and for an instant I could see that old woman raising holy hell with Hilda. It amused me, but I didn't dare laugh or even smile. Then Hilda sat down on the bed beside me and started thumping my chest with her fingers. She said her mother told her that American bomber pilots had had a saying, "Save One for Mainz." When they came back from missions deeper into Germany, they dropped whatever they had left on Mainz. When Hilda was a little girl, her mother had taken her all over the city to show her places that had been destroyed, piles of rubble that stayed on in Mainz for years after the war. Hilda's mother told her that just passing an American soldier on the street made her physically ill. "I tell you this," Hilda said, "but you don't know it."

"You don't know it either," I told her. "You weren't born yet. Then, I mean."

Hilda put her head down on my chest and was quiet.

When I drove her home, always late at night, she made me stop the car three blocks down the hill from where she lived. There was no traffic, there were not any pedestrians, at that time of night. But Hilda was brisk with me then, almost as if I were trying to keep her from going home. She got out of the car quickly after I stopped it, and began walking directly up the cobblestone street toward her mother's apartment. She kept the collar of her coat turned up, and she kept her coat cinched in tightly at her waist. With that way of walking she had, Hilda was very pretty to look at as she passed up that street, under the lights, and on away from me. She would turn and wave once before she went inside the gate and disappeared. Once or twice I drove up there and tried to guess which window was Hilda's, but I never knew for sure. That vision of her, lifting a hand at me from a long way off, was something I found so satisfactory that I sometimes sat long minutes in the car, forgetting where I was or where I had to go.

We often ate at *Gästhausen*. Hilda enjoyed eating, and we almost always found ourselves discussing food when we went out at night. I thought Hilda came closest to being a pretty woman when she sat down to eat; she fussed with the silver-ware, the cups and glasses; she arranged everything on the table just to suit her; she translated the menu for me, even the entries she knew wouldn't interest me. But it made her uncomfortable to be with me in a German place because of my short hair, my American clothes, and my American way of eating. She taught me to use my fork with only my left hand, and I had to admit that it was a logical way to get the food to your mouth. I liked going to those little village res-taurants that were filled up with the local folks who all knew each other. And I liked having Hilda order for me. But I could tell by her gestures and her way of talking, a little too prim and formal, that she was embarrassed to be with me in those places.

Once, to try to find a German place where Hilda could relax with me, I took her to one of the huge beer-halls in Frankfurt. A band was playing, and there were waitresses in dirndls carrying six and eight steins of beer at a time to the big tables. Hilda and I sat with half a dozen others, all Ger-mans, and the man beside me became very friendly with us; he kept telling Hilda that she looked like an angel, until finally she ignored him and kept her attention focused on the band and the crowd. The man's name was Dieter; so far as I could tell he spoke no English. Dieter asked me several questions, none of which I understood, but I ended up telling him that I was a *soldat*. Dieter put his arm around my shoulder and spoke with me at length. I understood none of what he said.

I was uncomfortable being hooked in so close to him. I kept bobbing my head, saying "*Ja, Ja,*" hoping he'd let me go. Dieter got out his wallet and gave a short speech over it, as if he intended to bless his money. Then he opened it and showed me a photograph of himself in military uniform, a shocking vision of Dieter as a boy. I saw the insignia on the collar, and I said it aloud, "SS?" He nodded his head and looked at me significantly. Then Hilda must have turned her attention back to us. She leaned across me and spoke to Dieter in rapid, crisp German. Dieter put his wallet away. He tried to argue with Hilda a couple of times, but she raised her voice and wouldn't hear him. He busied himself with getting the waitress's attention and ordering more beer for all of us at the table. Hilda continued speaking to him even though he ignored her. Then she said in English to me, "I'm ready to go, Reed." I protested; Dieter had just ordered beer for all of us. "Stay and drink his beer, if you like. I'm leaving," she said. I went with her. When I asked her why she had made such a scene, she said that Dieter had been acting and speaking improperly. She would not explain further than that. In the car, driving out of Frankfurt, Hilda and I argued with each other in a pleasant, familiar way.

I liked things to be rugged then. I was a paratrooper, after all. Every day I did extra push-ups, sit-ups, knee-bends. I jogged miles. I arm-wrestled with the first shirt and the company clerk. I irritated the old man, even though I knew it was a stupid thing to do. I wrote wild letters to my parents and my grandparents. One morning I typed out a request for an assignment to a combat unit in Vietnam; the old man smiled when I took it in to him. When I told Hilda that evening that I'd volunteered, she shook her head at me and said, "You're a stupid boy, aren't you?" She seemed amused by what I'd done, as if it were an antic, of which nothing much would come. But she didn't make me feel bad about it.

I became more confident of our relationship then. Since I was planning to leave, things seemed more settled between us. "Hilda, damn you," I'd say sometimes, just because I felt good, just to see if I could get a rise out of her.

"Then I'll be like you and your friends?" She'd lift an eyebrow at me. "No, thank you," she'd say, and she'd smile and run her hand over the short hair at the back of my head.

I did sometimes like to catch her off guard and tell her she had a bird in her head. Once when she'd shouted something at a car that almost ran over us near the casino in Wiesbaden, I asked her what she'd said. She told me she'd told the man he had a bird in his head. That tickled me. But once I said it to Hilda as a joke, and she blew up. If I really wanted to make her angry, all I had to do was tell her she had a bird in her head.

We had a terrible argument one night. I was tired, I admit it, but there was no excuse for Hilda to get into one of her moods. She was a very oral person, and she could be obsessive about biting. I did not want to be bitten that evening, and I told her so. She said several vile things to me. I think I was joking when I swung at her; I think I expected her to duck, the same way *I* would have done. But I popped her a good one, and her eye began to swell. I refused to drive her home. As I said, I was tired. She went outside, buttoning her blouse as she went, and yelled at me through the window. Then I dressed and went outside, too, and we yelled at each other in the parking lot until her taxi came. When I walked back into the B.O.Q., several of my fellow officers applauded from their windows.

A couple of days later, in the park, I met a suntanned American girl instructing a peacock to open its tail. She wanted to photograph it. Nancy came from a good family in Sedalia, Ohio, and she was an A student at Marietta College. Nancy was studying at Mainz University for the summer. She set her hair in curlers every morning. She smelled like girls I'd necked with in high school. She wore blouses with Peter Pan collars, and she wore circle pins; I put my finger in the circle and made Nancy blush with that old joke. Nancy planned activities, such as drives and picnics, to help us avoid "petting situations," as she called them. I was charmed. Nancy closed the door when she went to the bathroom; she even ran water in the sink. We drove along the Rhine and the Mosel, where I sampled the wines of the valleys, sitting at tables outside, getting myself dizzy and making my ears ring on sunny afternoons. We stopped at scenic places along the rivers and took pictures of each other with Nancy's camera. Sometimes we asked older German couples to take pictures of us together; then I put my arm around Nancy's waist and hugged her to me. We both smiled at the camera and at the bemused, helpful Germans.

Nancy worried about me the whole week I was scheduled to make my pay jump; she was happy when I came back from it all right. She asked me to tell her about parachuting. I taught her the nine jump commands; I showed her how to fall. Nancy started saying she wished I wouldn't go to Vietnam, she wished I would withdraw my request. I told her that what happened next was entirely out of my hands. Either I would go, or I would not go. I was thrilled by the sound of my voice when I told her that.

Then Nancy would spend the night with me if all we did was snuggle. She wore pajamas, underpants, and bra to bed. One night, at almost three in the morning, the phone rang. I crawled across Nancy to answer it.

"I want to see you," Hilda said.

"Hey, how are you doing?" I said.

"Are you busy?" Hilda spoke calmly, as if it were the middle of the day.

"It's pretty late. Why don't I call you back in the morning?"

"Tell her to get out." Hilda's voice took on an edge, and I got a little excited myself.

"Hilda, I won't be rude," I said.

"Good," she said. "I'm glad you won't be rude. I'm coming over there." Then I heard her laugh just before she hung up. I tried to figure out if she really would come over. I could see Hilda in the hallway, banging on my door with one of her shoes while Nancy wept in my bed.

"Who is Hilda?" Nancy asked.

"You don't want to know," I told her and knew immediately that she would think the worst. I stayed awake a long time wondering if Hilda was coming over. She was a crazy bitch. I couldn't think of anything she wouldn't do if she felt like it.

In August Nancy went back to Sedalia to get ready to go back to school. She wrote me twice a day. She sent snapshots of her parents, her little brother, her dog, and her roommate at Marietta. Nancy said they all said to say Hi to me. Nancy's parents had a swimming pool in their back yard, and Nancy sent a snap of herself in a bikini, with her hair wet and her hands at her hips, squinting at the camera. Penned across the back of it was *Don't I look horrible?* She was right. I began to throw the letters away without opening them.

I called Hilda at work and asked her to meet me.

At the restaurant Hilda was prim and reserved; she wore a pretty ruffled white blouse under her gray suit jacket. Her hair had been cut recently, and she was in a fine mood, I could tell, in spite of her formal manners. I told her to have whatever she wanted to eat, but she ordered only an omelet. I decided to be candid with her. I admitted I had acted badly toward her. She looked at her napkin. I told her about Nancy. She pursed her lips and said, yes, she had seen me once with a fat American girl, but she hadn't imagined romance between us. The girl had seemed an oaf, Hilda said. I said she was right. When I said it, I felt at that moment relieved of Nancy altogether.

Hilda sipped her coffee. She looked like a portrait of herself, a young woman musing in a restaurant, holding her cup between both her hands. I yearned for her then. She asked me if I would do a favor for her. She told me she'd been sleeping with an Infantry captain she knew I knew and detested. She was explicit and crude in her language, and I knew she was testing me, seeing if I would hold my temper. I forked rump steak into my face and didn't say anything.

Captain Jarvis—that was his name—had taken some pictures of Hilda. She wanted me to get them from him, along with the negatives. Captain Jarvis was married, and I knew it wouldn't be difficult to get the pictures from him.

"Why did you pose for him, Hilda?"

Her voice hit four clear notes: "He asked me to."

"Well, then why do you want the pictures back?"

"He says he might show them to Manfred." It was a complicated subject, and I could see that Hilda was willing to discuss it as long as I was interested. She ate small bites of her omelet and watched me. Through her eyes I saw myself: short-haired, awkward-mannered, inappropriately dressed. I felt nervous. I imagined myself in Sedalia, Ohio, at the swimming pool, hugging Nancy in her bikini, smiling at the camera, all teeth and ears and sunburnt nose and shoulders.

The next morning I called Captain Jarvis. It was fun, like acting in a movie. "Well, sir," I heard myself saying in velvet tones, "I'm sure you don't need advice from me. I'm sure you know where your best interests lie. The young lady tells me . . ." Oh, what a smooth one I was! And Jarvis was so polite and friendly and agreeable you'd have thought we were West Point classmates. That son of a bitch! An hour after the call, a P.F.C. delivered a sealed envelope to my office and asked me to sign a receipt for it.

The pictures amused me. I looked at them all the rest of that afternoon. Hilda was saucy in polka-dotted underpants with her hands on her hips and her pelvis stuck forward. Hilda lay flat on a bed with her hands daintily covering herself. Hilda held her left breast. Hilda poked her ass toward the camera. Hilda winked. Hilda was in color. When I had had enough of looking at them, I put the pictures back in the envelope and watched it turn dark outside my window. We were stationed in a cobblestone-paved German cavalry barracks, a place that seemed ancient to me. The two Airborne battalions were out jogging before evening chow, blocks of moving, shouting men in T-shirts and fatigue pants, their sergeants running beside the formations, calling out the songs: "You had a good home, but you left." Even when they had gone too far away for me to see them, I could still hear the men's voices, and after a while they began to sound like one powerful masculine voice chanting the cadences. I felt bad there in the dark office. I opened the envelope again and turned on my desk light.

That evening Hilda wore a tight black dress; she had on heavy blue eye-shadow and dark lipstick. She followed me around the room, pummeling at me, laughing. Finally I made her sit down in a chair. It took me a long time to tell her about how I sensed an unusually strong emotional connection between us, how I wanted us to talk more and to be serious with each other, not to make so many jokes. I wasn't sure what I meant to be telling her, but I knew that it made me feel like a fool to be pacing the floor in front of her, spouting off at the mouth while she picked at her nails, looked at her rings, and fixed her dress to lie exactly smooth over her legs. When I finished, she pursed her lips and examined me. "What do you think?" I asked her.

"Do you have the photographs?" she asked.

I told her I did.

"Good." She stood up. "Unzip me, please."

With her clothes puddled at her feet, her hands on her hips, and her chin jutting toward me, Hilda asked for the envelope, and I handed it over to her. She opened it to check the negatives and the pictures. Then she put it on the sofa. I liked seeing her breasts better when she bent over that way, when she wasn't so sure I was looking at them. She helped me undress. "Sit down," she said.

"No," I said. I tried to argue with her. "This isn't really what I want."

"Of course it isn't," she said and knelt on the floor in front of me. "Naturally it isn't what you want." She went ahead because she thought she knew what I wanted, but she didn't. I touched her hair with my hands. I felt tender toward her in spite of her being so wrong about me. "Hilda," I said, "I wouldn't have chosen this." But she didn't stop to answer me, and I didn't try to argue anymore.

"There," she said, when it was done, and laughed and sat back on her haunches. "Would you like more of that?" She was smiling in that way she had that made her features become ordered and her face almost pretty, but I felt as if I were seeing her from a distance.

"No," I said, "that's enough of that."

"Good," she said. She got up and went to her purse. She took out a cigarette, lit it, then stood up straight, dragging at it, puffing through her nostrils and looking at me through the smoke. She was aware that I was watching her, and she held herself proudly.

"I haven't seen you smoke before," I told her.

"It's something new with me," she said. "Do you like it?" She exhaled toward the ceiling.

"Sure," I said. "I think it's just fine."

Hilda went to the bathroom, sat down, and began to talk to me through the open door. She wanted to hold the cigarette in her teeth while she talked, but she wasn't practiced enough for it. She had to take it in her hand. Then she had to balance it on the sink.

"You know, Reed, you really are a pig," she said, pleasantly enough. It was her old self speaking, but there was something new in her voice.

I scooted down in the chair as far as I could go and looked up at the ceiling. "No, I'm not a pig, Hilda. Actually, I'm pretty decent, when you think about it. I got your pictures for you, didn't I?"

"But do you know how much I hate you?"

"You don't hate me, Hilda. You're crazy about me. You think I'm fantastic." I knew it was finished, but I figured I might as well try to keep the conversation civilized.

"I think you're a fantastic swine," she told me. The phrase pleased her. She stood up, flushed, and came out to kick through her clothes for what she wanted. She began to dress quickly, picking up things and jerking them on.

"Where are you going, Hilda?"

"To meet Manfred."

"Good old Manfred," I said.

Hilda bit her lip while she worked at the zipper behind her back. She took her purse and went to the mirror. She fixed her eye-shadow, her lipstick, and she hacked at her hair with a comb. She put her face very close to the mirror. Then she turned around and looked at me.

"Goodbye, fantastic swine," she said.

"Kraut bitch," I said. "Nazi whore," I said. She kept smiling and walked out into the hall. "Cocksucker," I shouted at her. She closed the door. I listened to her heels click-clack down the hallway. I should have remembered to tell her she had a bird in her head.

That's it. "I never saw her again" is the lousiest thing I know to say about somebody. A couple of times I wrote to Hilda from Vietnam. And then I wrote her about getting out of the army, coming home to Rosemary, and settling down with my parents to watch the tube "from news to news," as my father called it. I wrote her about driving all the way over to Madison for a beer and being the only one in the bar with short hair and the only one putting quarters in the jukebox. I wrote her about how, when the leaves began turning, my folks and the people down at Mrs. Elkins's store began talking about "the beautiful fall foliage," and how that made me feel desperate all day. I'd like to know what Hilda thought about those letters. She never responded, but I was certain she understood what I was telling her. I found myself feeling half homesick for Germany. I remembered going with Hilda into the Mainz Cathedral where there was a high space of dark, cool air over our heads and soft chanting all around us. I remembered that evening in Frankfurt, in the beer-hall, when Hilda had leaned across me to tell Dieter to put away his picture of himself as a young SS trooper. I knew I was being nostalgic and foolish. I wrote and confessed to Hilda that I had kept copies of those pictures Captain Jarvis had taken of her. I told her that if she answered my letters I would send the pictures to her. But I didn't expect that such a promise would shake her out of her silence. Hilda knew me perfectly well. She knew I would always keep one for myself.

Dirge

Notes

The Milkweed, the Mole Holes

The milkweed would unfold from its pods. When you broke off the pods, there was always a drop of white juice at the stem, which Duncan said was poison. We pressed the pods open and feathered out the silky white stuff inside. It made my hands smell. "That's enough," said Duncan, but I wanted more. We were on the front porch, it was a warm morning, and Duncan did not want me to break open any more of the milkweed pods we had picked and put into a white enameled bucket, full to the top. First my mother was out on the porch with us. Then my grandfather was there with her, and I was trying to tell them what was wrong, but I could not stop crying, could not make the words. Duncan told them, "He just wants more milkweed. That's all." Then he was offering me the whole white bucket full of pods, but I did not want it anymore, I could not stop the crying-out of my hurt throat, my hot face, and my grandfather was looking down at me and shaking his head.

The next time it was mole holes. Duncan and I were digging them in the corner of the yard. We pulled up the sod and the dirt that had been raised by the burrowing moles tunneling in our yard. Duncan and I laughed when we pulled up the earth and threw the chunks out away from us. We expected we would find a mole soon. I wanted to see one. Duncan and I met in the middle of a trench we had been working on from different directions. We laughed when we pulled the last piece of sod from it. While we were looking for new tunnels to start digging up, my mother came out and stopped us. She was mad about what we had done to the yard. Duncan didn't cry about it, but I started again. Mother went indoors, but soon she came back out again, this time with my grandfather. "See, he isn't hurt," she said, waving her hand toward me. "It's just mole holes this time," she said. "I made them stop digging up the lawn." She went indoors again, disgusted with me, but my grandfather stayed out there with us. Duncan pretended he was an older person watching me cry. My grandfather made us sit out there with him on the front porch steps. When I stopped crying, he said, "Damned if you can't make a noise, boy." He stayed out there a long while with Duncan and me on the porch steps.

At the Cistern

I walked the path across the field to my grandparents' house. It was summer, just before dark. They were both outside, my grandfather sitting down on top of the concrete cistern at the back of the house, my grandmother standing in front of him, in her white dress and stockings, with her

hands on her hips. He saw me first and said, "Hello, Reed."
My grandmother turned toward me and said, "Hello, Sonny."
Then she looked back down at my grandfather while she
kept talking to me. "What do you think of an old man who
has to fill himself up with liquor every evening to make
himself feel like a big shot?"

"Don't start that with the boy here," my grandfather said.
He was smoking and poking at the ash of the cigarette with
his little finger. The smoke rolled all around his hand, and
I got closer to him to be able to smell it.

"You old devil!" my grandmother said. "He ought to
know the truth about you. They'll tell him down at the post
office anyway."

"Stop it," said my grandfather. "Go indoors and listen
to your programs. Your programs are on now," he said.

My grandmother looked down on me and put her blue-
veined hand on my shoulder. "How do you like a drunkard,
Sonny? How do you like a drunkard?"

"Damn you," said my grandfather. "Damn you to hell,
old woman."

Shooting Crows

I sat with him in the field on the far side of his house,
the place where Duncan and I went sled-riding in the winter.
He held the shotgun in his lap and smoked, and we were
quiet when the condensing pattern of blackbirds came down
in the trees near us. The birds made a jingling sound in the
early-evening quiet. I nudged him and made motions for him
to hurry up, it would be dark soon. The sky was a cool
lavender color then, with the sunlight coming over the hill
from far behind us. He smoked down to the end of his cig-

arette, stubbed it out in the grass, while I fidgeted beside him. Then he lifted the gun, aimed it toward the tree full of birds, sighted carefully for a moment, and fired, the gun rocking him back. It was very loud. All the birds rose and angled out away from us, down toward the river, their wings making a vibrating noise for only a moment. "You got one!" I shouted. I had seen it fall. I was already running over that way.

It was flapping around in the grass and the milkweed when I got there, and there were spatters of blood on the leaves, but it was only twitching when I pushed the weeds out of the way to see it and nudged it with my toe. There were specks of blood on its mottled blue-black breast and neck, there was a thick drop coming from its beak. I picked it up by its tailfeathers and ran to take it to him. When he saw me coming, he shouted, "Drop that thing, Son! Don't bring that over here!"

"You shot a crow," I said, but I went ahead and dropped it like he told me. He had shot lots of times on other evenings, but he hadn't ever hit one before.

"It's not a crow," he told me. I walked toward him, leaving the dead bird in the broomsage behind me. "It's a starling," he said. He took a pint bottle from the jacket beside him, opened it, and turned it up to his mouth. "Ah," he said, as if the whiskey caused him pain. He wiped across his mouth with the khaki shirtsleeve, from the inside of his elbow to his wrist.

"May I have a sip of that, Granddad?" I asked him.

"Hell, no, Son," he said and put the cap back on. But then he handed the bottle to me and cautioned, "You better not take more than just a sip." I opened it and turned it up and let some of it go in my mouth. I was sorry that I did, because it burned. I wanted to spit it out, but I swallowed it, and it burned me so that I knew my eyes were tearing, but I didn't cough or anything. He took the bottle from me and put the cap back on. We heard the screen door slap shut. The white figure of my grandmother came out the back door. She stood on the cistern and shouted to us, "Elton, did you give that boy a drink of whiskey?"

"Hell, no!" my grandfather shouted. She stood out there and stared at us a while. Then she went back indoors. "Battle-ax," he muttered, "old battle-ax," and I giggled. We waited out there until it was almost full dark and he had finished the bottle. I didn't ask him for another sip, and he didn't offer one. He let me carry the shotgun back to the house, but when I started up the steps to go inside with him, he took the gun from me and told me to go on home.

Horns

I had a trumpet I'd bought with money earned from my paper route. My father ordered it for me from the classified ads in the Roanoke paper. The trumpet was a concert instrument, a little more slender than an ordinary trumpet, a little sharper in tone. It was plated with real gold, and its valve action was fast and light. I played that trumpet, and I played my father's alto saxophone. I went into my grandparents' parlor, where there was the upright Steinway piano, and there I practiced either the saxophone or the trumpet while they were upstairs, my grandfather drinking bourbon from a water glass in the bathroom, leaning against the sink, with his hat on, and my grandmother standing in the door of the bathroom, harping at him about his drinking.

When Cassie called them down for dinner, I went into the dining room with them to sit and talk. My grandfather's face was flushed. He was cheerful, though my grandmother was gloomy and quiet at the beginning of the meal. My grand-father told me about the days when he played the alto horn in the Rosemary town band. It was hard for me even to imagine that there ever was such a band. He told me how he knew only one tune, "There'll Be a Hot Time in the Old Town Tonight," and he stopped eating long enough to try to whistle the tune for me. He was tone-deaf, and he'd never learned how to whistle very well, and so I couldn't make out how the song went, but my grandfather was eager for me to learn it and play it for him. My grandmother told him to go on eating his dinner and be quiet. He continued talking, telling me how he would take me to Roanoke or to Bristol very soon, and he would buy me a cornet. He said that a cornet had a much sweeter and more mellow sound than the trumpet I had been playing. My grandmother again told him to be quiet and to go on eating his dinner, that Cassie had to wash the dishes and go on down the hill to her house before it got dark.

My grandfather described the shape of the cornet, explain-ing that it was rounder and shorter than a trumpet, and said that he would buy me a gold-plated one because he thought they were the best looking. "I promise you that's exactly what I'll do, Sonny," he said, and I wondered why it was of such importance to him that he promised like that. But I wanted a cornet to go with my trumpet and the saxophone that my father had turned over to me. When he talked like that about the cornet, I could almost see the horn in its velvet-lined case. My grandmother told him to go on with his dinner, and my grandfather told her to go to hell. She called him a drunkard, and he called her an old devil, and she said *he* was the old devil. Then they appealed to each other to stop it because I was there at the table. But I didn't care what they said, I was thinking about how the three instruments would look lined up in front of me.

Great-Grandmother

My father carried my great-grandmother from the car, up the steps into the yard that was overgrown with honeysuckle, up the steps to the porch, up a step into her house, and then up the scary staircase that had no bannister to the second floor, and around that hallway into her bedroom. When he was carrying her up that way, my great-grandmother clutched at her nightgown and told him that she didn't want to show her rear end. When my father had caught his breath, which took him a long time, he chuckled softly about that.

Before she had to go to the hospital my great-grandmother had corns on her feet that my grandmother filed with sand-paper sticks in the kitchen after every Sunday dinner, while Cassie stood at the sink and washed dishes. When my great-grandmother cried out, my grandmother stopped her filing. My great-grandmother said that my grandmother was trying to hurt her, and my grandmother said that she wasn't. They bickered some, then they sat in there for a while without saying anything, both of them gazing out the windows, and then they started the filing again. The afternoon passed slowly that way until it was time for my father to take my great-grandmother to her own house down in the center of Rosemary.

She lived there with my Aunt Inez, who was crazy, according to my grandmother on my mother's side and my great-aunt Pat. Sometimes I would see Aunt Inez going out of the kitchen toward the hallway. She had gray hair. She cut herself sometimes and saved the bandages. She wore rags.

Once when my father had finished talking on the phone and my mother asked him what was wrong, my father said, "Why, Grandma Weston is going to die." But she didn't die that time or this time either. She was home from the hospital.

My father sat there talking with her while he caught his

breath. She wanted him to get her snuff for her, to get the bowl she spit in. Aunt Inez passed by the door once and then again going the other way, but she didn't look in or come into the room. "Hello, Inez," my great-grandmother called out, but Aunt Inez didn't answer. She was wearing a T-shirt and men's overalls. She walked stooped over, as if she were carrying something heavy. Aunt Inez never talked to anybody much, except my grandfather. He sometimes came down there and sat with her in the kitchen.

My grandmother waited for us in the car. When we came down from my great-grandmother's house and got back in the car with her, she wanted my father to tell her everything. He tried to make her feel all right. My grandmother was my great-grandmother's daughter, and she was my father's mother, and Aunt Inez was my grandmother's baby sister. Turning into the driveway to our house and my grandmother's house, my father and my grandmother began singing a hymn, she taking the alto part. This was just at twilight. I had never heard them sing before, either of them.

Threshing Wheat

Peaks was the foreman. He drove the truck, and my grandfather sat up front with him. They offered me the middle of the front seat, but I wanted to sit in the back of the truck, in the open air, with Monkey, Hitler, and Crow Jim. Hitler and Crow Jim made their own cigarettes with Prince Albert tobacco. They smoked as if it were their greatest pleasure.

Monkey smiled at me. He called me Honey, and he called Duncan that, too, but Duncan didn't like it. Monkey was Church of God, and at lunchtime he went off by himself and prayed. He had grown up with my father; they'd caught fish together and put them in the reservoir down below our house.

The dirt road out to the farm was rough. When it bumped us in the back of the truck, Crow Jim said, "That son of a bitch." He said the truck made his back hurt and Peaks knew it. He said he was going to smack the shit out of Peaks one of these days. I looked at Peaks through the window in the back of the truck cab. He was saying something, very seriously, to my grandfather, but I couldn't hear him. Crow Jim was small and dark. He and Monkey smelled a way that my mother said came from not taking baths, but Crow Jim smelled like cigarettes, too. My grandfather would look at Crow Jim and say, "James King, better known as Crow Jim," and Crow Jim would shift his eyes all around and say, "Yes sir, Mr. Bryant." He almost smiled when he answered my grandfather, but that was about as close as he ever came to it.

When we ran inside the gate to my grandfather's farm, Peaks driving through and stopping to wait for me while I swung the old wooden contraption shut behind the truck, I rode the last little distance on the running board, with my grandfather holding on to my jacket. Then I ran to the pipe where the spring water came out, and took a drink. Whenever Duncan and my mother and father and I drove out to the farm, this was what we always did first, took a drink of the spring water, but now none of the others came to the pipe with me.

Once, trying to clean the old wooden threshing machine up so that it would work, Crow Jim had crawled under it, and, lying down on his back, had opened a hatch that dumped a load of chicken manure into his face. Now Peaks started the tractor and backed it up to the new threshing machine. The new one was painted a bright orange. It was as big as my grandmother's kitchen and front porch put together. It had pulleys and belts, a ramp in back of it, and a big pipe that folded up on top but that could be swung down. Peaks made the tractor bellow. Then he pulled the threshing machine out into the light. All of us looked at that thing, watched it sway as Peaks pulled it down the dirt road and across the cattle-guard.

From a distance the field seemed a smooth brown that would be soft to walk on with your bare feet, but when we were in it and down off the pickup, I saw that it was covered with brittle stubble. Sheaves of wheat were stacked in shocks every fifty or seventy-five yards. Just inside the gate, the others were there waiting for us: Mr. Delby and Jim, Old Man Richardson and two of his sons. It was hot already. The men rolled up their sleeves while they were talking, and I took off my jacket.

A long, wide belt was stretched from a pulley on the tractor to a pulley on the threshing machine. Another pulley on a lever tightened the belt so that the threshing machine ran. It shook and clattered and made a terrific noise. Looking at it when Peaks started it, Mr. Delby smiled over at my grandfather and shook his head admiringly. Peaks worked the tractor and the threshing machine. He knew how my grandfather's machines worked.

The Richardson boys took their small tractor and their flat-bedded wagon out into the field to gather the sheaves of wheat and haul them back to the threshing machine. Old Man Richardson stayed at the open end of the machine and helped them feed the wheat into it. From the high ramp at the back, straw rolled up and out of the machine in a graceful curving arc to the ground. Jim Delby and Hitler and Monkey were back there with pitchforks to stack it up around a high pole stuck in the field.

Crow Jim and I were stationed at the end of the pipe where the wheat came down out of the machine. We had a stack of burlap bags beside us. There were hooks at the end of the chute to hold up one side of the bag; I held up the other side with my hands until it was full. Then we closed off the chute for a moment and changed bags. Together Crow Jim and I could lug a full bag of wheat over to my grandfather's pickup truck. He and Mr. Delby were there, sitting on the running board, on the shady side, talking. Mr. Delby got up each time to help us heft the bag of wheat into the bed of the truck. Then he went back to talking with my grandfather, who smoked and fanned himself with his hat and cautioned me not to hurt my back lifting those bags.

I heard Jim Delby whooping, Crow Jim gave me a nudge in the ribs and pointed, and I turned to see Hitler with a writhing blacksnake in his hands, chasing Monkey out across the stubbly field. I asked Crow Jim where the snake came from—I imagined it flying up out of the machine with the straw—but Crow Jim shrugged and said, "Watch." Hitler stopped there out in the field, a good distance from us, and then Monkey stopped, too, and watched Hitler from even farther out in the field. Hitler waited until he had the hold he wanted on the snake. Then he let it fly out away from him like a rope. He flapped it once, then cracked it like a whip, twice, the second time very hard. The snake was limp then, hanging straight down from his hand. Hitler laughed and threw the thing at Monkey, who dodged away from it.

Crow Jim put his dark hand under the stream of grain coming down from the chute out into the burlap bag I held. He put a handful of grain into his mouth and began to chew it, grinning at me out of his moving mouth. I took a handful, too. The grains crunched under my teeth; then they turned into something the texture of bread dough or chewing gum. All the rest of the day I kept swallowing a little of it and adding more grains of wheat into my mouth to chew.

At lunchtime, the men took their dinner-buckets from the cab of the pickup and went to sit in the shade at the far side of the threshing machine. Monkey went off by himself, far over to the other side of the field; soon we heard him praying, shouting at the top of his voice, but he had hidden from us, behind an old blasted apple-tree stump, so that we wouldn't see him kneeling out there.

My grandfather called me over to sit with him and Peaks on the running board of the truck. He opened first a can of sardines, curling the top off with the long key that came stuck to the can. Then he used his pocketknife to open three small cans of pork and beans. Under the seat of the truck he had a square box of saltine crackers, and in the glove compartment he had some plastic forks for us to use. "Slow down, Son," he told me, and Peaks laughed and spit cracker crumbs. My grandfather opened a second can of sardines, using his pocket-knife to scoop them out of the can and slide them onto the saltine crackers; he passed them to Peaks and me.

The men lay under the threshing machine. We could hear the steady murmur of one or two of them talking and then their loud laughter coming up every so often. Peaks spread his long body down on the ground there by the truck and talked to my grandfather. My grandfather told about a hotel in Kingsport, Tennessee, where he'd stayed years ago and about the restaurant where he ate and about the waitress who always looked after him.

Every cloud was gone from the sky after lunch, and the sun was strong enough to feel through your shirt. The men were soaked with sweat, wet to their shirt collars, their hat brims, even in patches at the crotches of their overalls. The pickup truck had taken in one load of the burlap sacks of wheat; we were almost through a second load. Monkey was at the top of the stack of straw, near the top of the pole, working hard to keep pace with Hitler and Jim Delby, who forked up thick bunches of straw for him to place at the top. While I was watching, they threw forkloads of straw directly on him. Then they did it again. I saw Monkey throw his pitchfork off the stack onto the ground, saw him slide down to where Hitler and Jim were trying not to laugh about what they had done. Monkey screamed at them, "Stop it! Stop it! Stop it!" He didn't curse, and what he shouted sounded silly. He came away from them and walked around the pickup truck where my grandfather sat and where Peaks stood with his foot cocked up on the front bumper. "Oh Lord," Monkey said. "Oh Lordy!" Peaks talked to him but had a grin at the corners of his mouth. Then my grandfather talked to him. Then Monkey went back up on the stack of straw and worked hard to catch up with all the straw he had to place up there. The men who did that work, all three of them, had chaff and small pieces of straw stuck to their clothes and their arms, necks, and faces.

Peaks asked Crow Jim to hold the bags while I rested. I told him that I wasn't tired, but he told me, "Get your ass over to that truck and talk to your granddaddy," and I went ahead and did it. My grandfather made me sit with him for ten full minutes, timing it on his pocket watch, before I could go back to holding the sacks at the grain chute. He told me that I should have worn a hat.

Crow Jim and I were both tired. We could hardly lug the sacks of wheat across the short distance to the pickup truck. My arms were heavy. And then finally we were finished with it. The field was done. The tractor was shut off. The threshing machine stopped its enormous noise. The silence was all around us. Peaks straightened up from the belt he was pulling off the threshing machine. He pointed. Down out of the woods at the top of the field came a deer, running almost directly at us, a buck with a rack of antlers, five or six points on each side. The deer turned away once, running sideways to us now, so that we could see how it moved, and when it came to the fence, it rose off the ground so slowly and lightly that it was more like floating than jumping. We heard dogs yapping back up in the woods. After the deer had gone on down the next field and across the road into those woods over there, the dogs streamed down out of the woods above us. The dogs were frantic, stretched out running, with their tongues lolling back out of the sides of their mouths.

In the back of the truck, going home, Crow Jim and Hitler and I stood with our backs leaning against the cab. Monkey sat hunkered down against the side, looking back away from us. Hitler and Crow Jim teased Monkey. They said they knew what he was thinking when he jumped off that haystack and shouted at Hitler and Jim Delby. Monkey shook his head and didn't say anything to them. Then he unbuttoned the top pocket of his overalls bib. He took out a small New Testament, with red edges to the pages and a pebbled black plastic cover. He began to thumb the pages. I could see the columns of red and black lettering on the white pages. Monkey and Crow Jim turned around to face into the wind. "Who are you going to get to read that thing to you?" asked Hitler, turning back once to look down at Monkey. Hitler was Monkey's brother, and he knew he couldn't read. "I know what it says," said Monkey. He thumbed the pages. "I know what it says," he said.

TV

The old man walked across the field to watch TV at our house. Over at his house my grandmother would be sitting in the straight-backed chair in the study, nodding her head with her eyes closed, while the Madison radio station played its last hour of music, usually the Silver Strings of Mantovani or Andre Kostelanetz and the Orchestra.

"Gunsmoke" was what my grandfather would have preferred to have every evening on TV, but he would take what he could get. He came in without knocking, speaking baby-talk to Missy, our mongrel dog. He passed through the unlighted dining room. "Hello, Pap," said my father, without getting up from his chair. "Hello, Granddad," said my mother from the couch, and Duncan and I from our chairs said it, too.

"Hello, Elton. Hello, Miriam," he said to my parents while he was taking off his jacket and hat. "You sorry scutters!" he said to Duncan and me, and he settled into the chair that we kept free for him. If someone were sitting there when he came in, he would refuse to take it and would sit in one of the straight-backed dining-room chairs, far back in that dark room. So Duncan and I got into the habit of staying out of his chair when we knew he was coming over to watch TV. From his pocket he took a flat pillbox that he used for an ashtray and set it out on the arm of the chair. He wouldn't use an ashtray in our house because he knew my father had given up cigarettes and my mother didn't like smoking. When he lit a cigarette in our house, he cupped it in his hand as if he could keep my mother from knowing what he was doing that way. He smoked the butts of the Camels down until they were about to burn his lips. Then he crushed them into the pillbox until they were flat as dimes. At the end of the evening, he folded the box up and put it in his pocket, waiting until he was out in the field between our house and his before he emptied it.

My mother liked to say something every evening about how

proud she was that he had stopped drinking, and my grandfather shook his head whenever the subject came up, as if he
had lost a thing that he valued greatly. Doc was his favorite
character in "Gunsmoke," or on all of TV for that matter.
My grandfather claimed that Doc made him think of old Dr.
Clark, who had been both a drunkard and a morphine addict
and for whom my grandfather had worked as an assistant many
years before in Rosemary. The scenes in "Gunsmoke" that
featured Doc and Kitty in the saloon were my grandfather's
favorites, and he usually spoke directly to the television set at
the end of those scenes. "That's exactly what I say, Doc," he
would say, and my father would look over and say, "Old
Doc's about to get in trouble now, isn't he, Pap?" I could tell
that it pleased my father for my grandfather to come to our
house and watch TV. My grandfather each night reminded
my father that it was time to feed the dog her M&M's, and
they chuckled at the dog's antics.

"Why, it's a goddamn commercial," my grandfather said.
He had difficulty making the transition between the program
narratives and the words from the sponsors. Duncan and I
would help him get straightened out sometimes. When he
walked back across the field, we could look out the window
in the study and see his flashlight moving through the dark.

Shaving

In my jump boots, starched khaki uniform, and overseas
cap, I walked into the empty kitchen, went through the fresh
cream-smelling pantry to the hallway. The study where they
both sat after dark and where he sat most of the day now was
empty, light falling across the chairs and sofa and the worn
Oriental rug on the floor. This was the room where I had

last seen him, more than a year before, and it was incorrect for him not to be there now when I had come back. "Anybody home?" I called out while I stood in the hallway. Then I heard steps upstairs.

"Up here!" my grandmother called out. I started up the front steps, rounding the newel post on top of which two brass cherubs struggled to hold up a lantern, and saw my tiny grandmother coming to meet me. "We're up here, Son," she said. I came up and bent down to her and kissed her. She was distracted, her brow furrowed, her mouth shaping words that wouldn't quite come to her. I might have been gone only a day or two. I was the grandchild whose face and ears she washed when I came here summer mornings. "Ah, Lord, we're in a mess here," she said. "Come in here and see what a mess we're in."

I followed her into the bathroom. My grandfather had pulled a chair in there to face the sink, and he was sitting in the chair, bending forward, facing the huge mirror, trying to shave. I started to tease him about sitting down to shave, but then I didn't say anything, because I saw what he had become. He was in his undershirt, his suspenders hanging on his pants down around his hips. He was thin, almost skinny. Even his bald head looked smaller, and his neck was that of an emaciated man. "Who is it?" he asked, turning to me. His spectacles were sitting on the sink. I didn't blame him for being angry at somebody who would come to visit him and catch him like that.

"It's Reed, Granddad," I told him. I tried not to gawk at him. Even his voice seemed to have lost its timbre. He turned back to what he was doing. His hand was shaking when he tried to put the razor to his face. There were splotches of shaving soap and dots of blood on his jaw, neck, chin, lips.

"Hello, Reed," he said. "I'm trying to shave. Cutting the

shit out of myself is what I'm doing, though."

"Yes sir, I can see that," I said. I sat down on the edge of the bathtub to watch him. I could see, too, that the situation tickled him some. "You want me to do that for you, sir?"

"Hell, no!" he said and turned his droll face to me. "If it was up to me, wouldn't cut her at all, would just let her grow till she hit the floor. But that one"—he jerked his head back toward the hallway behind him, by which he meant to indicate my grandmother—"that one out there has been on me about it all this week. 'Gotta shave, gotta shave,' " he mimicked. "I'd rather cut my goddamn jaw off than listen to that all day."

"Yes sir," I said.

He half stood up from the chair, leaned forward, and commenced splashing water on his face. Then he stopped and looked over at me, blinking his eyes. "I thought you were in Germany, Reed," he said.

"I was, sir. I'm back here for a little while before I have to go somewhere else."

My grandmother came in then and stood behind him. "Now just look at him," she said and turned to me with her look of suffering. "That's what he's come to. Your granddaddy," she said.

"No goddamn worse than you, old woman," he said. He went back to splashing water on himself. My grandmother walked out into the hallway again, shaking her head as she went.

When he'd dried himself off, he put on his spectacles and turned to examine me. "By God," he said. "Look at you. You got a hat?" he asked, and I showed him that I did. "Put that on," he said. "Let's see how you look."

I put on the hat, angled it just right, stood up, and came to attention for the old man.

Grandmama's Hell

"I wish you would look," my grandmother said, standing at the stove, stirring her tea, "at this hell I live in."

"Yes, ma'am," I said. I sat at the kitchen table to watch her, to meet the steady stare of her blue eyes. The state of my grandmother's house, the absence of the servants she had once had, and the wretchedness of national politics were the dominant aspects of what she called the hell she lived in, of which she considered my grandfather and President Roosevelt the authors. The dining-room table and the chairs around it were covered with newspapers, the room's sliding doors closed on it. Sheets covered the three black rocking chairs and the black leather easy chair in the parlor. Cassie wasn't able to come up the hill to work for my grandparents anymore. The quality of my grandmother's life had been declining, and she had been furiously bitter about it, for as long as I could remember. In the study, on the mantel, there was a picture of her in a dress of the twenties, very stylish-looking, and with something like a turban on her head, an expression of pride on her face; she said that photograph had been taken in New York. I would not have known the woman in the picture was her, except that I had been told so. Aside from the one of her with my father in his sailor suit—in which neither of them looked like the people I knew—that was the only picture of her to be seen in the house. Sometimes Duncan or one of her nieces, nephews, or cousins, bringing a camera over to her house, would take a picture of her and then mail it to her later. My grandmother was happy to pose for such pictures, but when they came to her in the mail she laughed ruefully over how she looked in them and put them away.

From the kitchen I heard my grandfather coming slowly down the front steps into the hallway. I waited until I knew he had settled himself into his chair in the study. "I'll go and talk to him for a while now," I said. My grandmother followed me through the pantry into the hall.

"Yes, you go and talk to him," she said from behind me, "because he may not be around much longer." She was almost yelling that last, because she wanted him to hear it. My grandmother had been discussing my grandfather's coming death in his presence for the last several years, as if it were something she was certain he had in mind to do to make her life more hectic.

Blood Flakes

My grandfather sat in the study with his back to the window. His cigarette was already lit, though he had just sat down, and layers of blue smoke rose in slow swirls around him. He hunched over, his elbows on the arms of his chair, his mouth working at the cigarette, pulling the smoke down into his lungs. The cut places on his pink face were small spots of dried brown blood; he would rub the flakes off his face for the rest of the day. Mid-morning sun beamed down through the latticed windows, stripes of yellow light falling across his shoulders, his pink head.

"Do you want that light on, Reed?" he asked me.

I told him that I didn't, that I liked the study just that way. I sat in the disintegrating black leather easy chair, patched with Scotch tape years ago, so that even the tape was now turning into powder. It was supposed to be his chair, but he had never liked it, never would sit in it, preferred the straighter-backed rocker that would let him face the library table like a desk, where he could lay open the back issues of railroad magazines or the medical books or the engineering texts that he got from the correspondence course that he took.

In his clothes now, he didn't look so frail as he had upstairs shaving. I could almost imagine him back to the man he was. My grandfather had always had a big belly on him, though his arms and legs weren't fat. He was bald from the first sight of him I could remember, his head shiny and pink beneath the hat that he didn't take off unless manners required it of him but that he had off now on my account. He was still dressed in khaki shirt and pants that now fit him too loosely, the pants folded at the waist and safety-pinned, the belly and crotch of them, which would have been stretched tight across his belly in the old days, now pooching up in empty folds.

When he was drunk of an evening, in those days when I would come over here to his house to play the piano or the trumpet or the saxophone in the parlor, then, when I came into the study here, with Grandmama sitting in front of the radio nodding to the music or to Lowell Thomas's news, my grandfather would be sitting at this library table with an old envelope in front of him, writing figures, equations, words, making small drawings or diagrams. If I asked him what he was working on, he would shove the envelope aside, stick it into a pile with a dozen others like it, and say that he was just trying to remember something he'd forgotten. And before, when I would start to sit down in that chair to face him, before my butt would have even touched down, he would have started the teasing, "You sorry scutter! You got the look of somebody who's been chasing split-tails, somebody who's been calling up the split-tails and talking to them on the telephone."

Now he looked at me, and his face was like an old dog's.

Optometry

My grandparents bickered only halfheartedly at dinner,

the summer light streaming through the kitchen windows onto the table where we ate. My father's company had assigned him to work a year in Louisville; they were closing the Rosemary carbide plant. My grandfather and grandmother both seemed saddened, a little bewildered by the absence of my mother and father in the house across the field, which was rented for the year now to Jim Delby, his wife and twin daughters. On this visit I did not go over there, but now and then I found myself at a window staring across the field at the white side of that house, the windows of its bedroom upstairs and the study below it. Most of the afternoon my grandfather had been discussing with me a trip we would take tomorrow, to Madison, to see the optometrist so that he could get a new pair of glasses.

Toward the end of dinner, my grandmother instructed him that he was to drive the truck down into Rosemary tomorrow to pick up the mail and to go to the store. My grandfather refused, said that Monkey would pick up the mail and bring it to her, at which time she could tell him what she wanted from the store, and Monkey would bring that to her the next day. My grandmother said that Monkey was unsatisfactory, that my grandfather himself had to go, had to drive the truck down there. Although I knew better, I interceded, pleading my grandfather's case, saying that our trip to the optometrist's was what had to be accomplished tomorrow morning before I began the long trip out to Louisville.

My grandmother gave her mean laugh when I tried to convince her that the trip to Madison was important. My grandfather was physically weak; his vision was terrible. I could hardly imagine his even getting the truck started and backed out of the garage, let alone driving it down into Rosemary. He chuckled about it and said that people down there got out of his way when they saw him coming, but I could see that he didn't want to drive that truck. My grandmother told me, "He's got to keep going," and my grandfather looked uncomfortable. When I insisted that he and I were going to Madison to see the eye doctor tomorrow morning, that I was driving him in their car, she said, "All right, Son," and she gave me a look that I knew was intended to be full of significance.

That night I slept in their guest room with its brass bed, its smell of the cedar chest where my grandmother kept things that were valuable to her, its silver powder-box that played a waltz when you lifted up the lid. This was the room where my grandmother did her exercises in the morning, willing herself to lift her five-pound barbells, to do the sit-ups, the leg-lifts, the women's push-ups, with her knees on the floor instead of her toes, and even to stand on her head. Before I went to sleep, I thought about the story both my father and my grandfather had told about her, never in her presence and always with a kind of awe of her. My father had gone out to play in the new sailor suit she'd bought him, he'd gotten it dirty playing in mud, she'd found and begun switching him, apparently losing her head, so that my grandfather had to come down from his toolshop to stop her. And I thought, too, about the old mystery that Duncan and I speculated about, the bullet holes my father, when he was a teenager, had put in the mirror of the closet-sized wardrobe in my grandparents' bedroom.

It was hard for me to see my father as the child in the sailor suit, the grown boy shooting the mirror. Easier was the vision of him answering the phone, about the time I was two or three years old, and obeying my grandmother's request, that he walk over there and talk my grandfather out of leaving her. That story was my mother's, and in it I was able to see my father clearly, sitting on one of the twin beds while my grandfather packed his suitcase on the other one, the two of them talking, my grandfather upset and shouting, my father trying to be calm, reasonable.

In the morning my grandfather and I left the house before my grandmother came downstairs. It was a warm, fragrant day. My grandfather looked out the car window at the new houses going up in Cedar Springs, the new highway overpass half constructed at Fort Ellis. When I objected to what the highway people were doing to the farmland there, my grandfather advised me that it would make traveling easier for the newer, faster cars. In Madison I parked the car and helped him out. I could see a trace of his old public way of walking, a kind of countryman's swagger he affected, or at least a walk that gave anybody to know that the old man had come to town and that he had money in his pocket.

Dr. Rosenberger lectured my grandfather gently over the business of his not having had an eye examination for more than thirty years. My grandfather had a kind of whining servility that he put on with such men as the optometrist. Over and over he said, "Yes, sir, Doctor, I know you're right. You're absolutely right about that, sir."

When we left the optometrist's, my grandfather was tired, and he took the arm I offered him, then steered me in the direction of the state liquor store. I helped him get the half a block or so up there, and I teased him about the eye doctor's office being so near to the liquor store, but he acted like he didn't hear me.

We came in the door of that place, and my grandfather let go of my arm. He looked like he'd have thrown away his cane if the thought had occurred to him. One clerk, behind the counter, down at the end of a line of furtive-faced whiskey-buyers and winos, saw him and spoke up, "Why, hello there, Mr. Bryant," and then another one over beside that one, and even the third one, who was a young man and probably didn't remember my grandfather, nodded at him respectfully. It was as if my grandfather had come home. He ordered five fifths of I.W. Harper bourbon and laid two crisp twenties down on the counter. While the one clerk rang up the purchase and packaged the bottles, each bottle in a separate paper bag twisted at the top and then all five of them in a large double bag, the other clerk came up to ask my grandfather where he'd been and how he was getting along. I took the bag for him while he put his change away, and we went out of the store, he taking my arm on the sidewalk. He was puffing by the time we got to the car, but I could tell he was in a fine mood. He told me to put the whiskey in the trunk, told me to put it as far back as I could so that my grand-mother couldn't find it.

But she was waiting for us there on the back porch, asking if we had gone to the liquor store. She asked both of us, knowing it would be harder for me to lie to her. I said, "We went to the optometrist's." But she knew the evasion, knew, too, that my grandfather was straight-out lying. When we went in the house, she went upstairs, got her keys, came back down and walked up to the garage. My grandfather made his way back through the house to the study, as if he didn't care what the old woman did, but I stood outside on the back porch and watched her bring out the package from the garage, go out behind the garage where there was a pile of stones my grandfather had intended to use for building something years before, so long ago that the whole pile was covered with honeysuckle now. And though I couldn't see her doing it back there, I could hear the bottles breaking from where I stood. When she came down the hill and up onto the porch, out of breath, she told me, "You don't have to take care of him when he's had a drink. You don't have to try to lift that man up off the floor and get him into bed."

All three of us tried to pretend, as I was going out to the car to go to Louisville, that what had happened hadn't happened. I shook hands with him, and I kissed her cheek.

"You'll come back home soon?" she said.

"Home?" I said, but as soon as I said it I knew she was right, and she was looking at me with her level, pale, blue-eyed gaze. This was where I was going to keep on coming back to again and again.

"Yes, Grandmama," I said, "I'll be here soon."

The Flatted Third

"I don't believe it," said Janie when she got in the car I had rented. She had just now come out of the building where she worked, on Thirty-ninth Street, and I could see she was upset, would cry any time now.

"I do," I said. The traffic wasn't bad this time of the early afternoon. I was already in the flow of cars heading into the Lincoln Tunnel before she answered me.

"Mr. Hardnose," she said. Then we were down into the tunnel with the shivering fluorescent light and the singing roar of car and truck tires all around us. "We saw him playing with Burt." Burt was Duncan's and Eleanor's two-year-old, and Janie made me angry calling up the vision of the old man playing with that baby while I was trying to drive the goddamn car through the goddamn tunnel. I looked at her and started to say something but then didn't. Janie turned around in the seat to address the dog, who was pacing and trembling in the back seat. "It's all right, Preacher," she crooned to him. "We'll be out of this tunnel soon."

We came up out of it, making the sharp, circling curve around to enter the New Jersey Turnpike, four lanes of traffic narrowing down to three. It was a gray day, the whole sky pewter-colored, but it was certain it wouldn't rain, and it wouldn't clear up for the rest of that February afternoon.

"He was all right then," Janie said, still petting the dog, trying to get him to lie down back there.

"You talking to me or that dog?" I asked her, but she didn't say anything. So after a while I told her, "You don't know if he was all right or not. You didn't know him except when he was old and sick. He stopped being all right five years ago. Ten years ago."

"Stop it, Reed," Janie said.

"All right," I said, and I really was sorry then. We were out of the city and rolling through that nasty, blasted factory landscape of what we called the Jersey flats, but I felt released, moving toward something, no longer aggravated. The old man had cared for Janie, so that he would talk to her, would focus his attention on her whenever she and I went over there, and would seem to brighten and become sharp-witted again in conversation with her. She'd sit in the study with him and Grandmama, the two of them asking her questions about what kind of life we lived in the city and did her parents want to become grandparents and what were we going to do when I finished graduate school. I'd get tired of that talk and would go through the door into the parlor to bang on the piano while they kept right on going.

"It's an old habit," I told her. "Duncan and I were fighting over whose grandfather he was from the time I can remember anything at all about him."

"You wanted him all for yourself," Janie said, and I nodded. "Still do, don't you?" she asked. The notion startled me so much that I had to think about it a while.

"I don't know what I want now," I said. "Maybe to go back"—we smiled at each other about that phrase, one we both used in certain conversations—"to go back to playing Monopoly on the Oriental rug there in the parlor with some of Grandmama's incense burning in the Buddha's lap on the mantel and with me having Boardwalk and Park Place with hotels on them and a stack of five-hundred-dollar bills and Duncan mad as hell about it, telling them all in the study that I had cheated but both of us knowing that I hadn't, and then hearing that old man laugh in there, that great big laugh of his that rolled out of him."

Janie smiled and let her head go back to rest against the seat, let her eyes fall shut against the dull glare of the afternoon. I almost reached over to smooth the fine dark hair away from her temple. Janie would listen to my talking about my childhood for days on end without ever stopping, just the same as I would listen to her if she was telling about hers, too. I thought she could see me clearly back in the past, as an eight-year-old, say, with a cowlick, my shirt untucked and a runny nose, standing up at the old man's desk in the back of his toolshop, pestering him for a piece of chewing gum. Janie was quiet for such a long time that I thought she was asleep, but then she spoke up, still keeping her eyes closed, "What if he had gone with Duncan and Eleanor that time? You couldn't have stood that, could you?"

"He'd have never done it," I said. "It was just a notion they had. They never even really asked him." About a year before, Duncan and Eleanor had gone over there with the kids, and they were shocked at how Grandmama treated him, always nagging at him, getting him to go out and do this or that or go up to the shop, or calling him names, the same things she'd been doing for all of Duncan's and my life and a long time before we were even born. Duncan and Eleanor asked Janie and me what we thought about their taking the old man to live with them. "They wanted to save him from

Grandmama," I told her, "but they knew the same thing I did—"

"We did," Janie corrected me.

"—we did, that she was keeping that old man alive. Hell, his hip hurt him, and his shoulders hurt him, and he didn't have an appetite and couldn't eat anything decent even if he did have one. He couldn't take a sip of liquor without it going straight to his brain and knocking him out. He couldn't half see, and he was taking a fall every couple of weeks and banging the shit out of himself. He was ready to give it up and sit there in that chair in the study and read railroad magazines until he rotted."

"Yes," Janie said, her eyes open now, looking out ahead at what New Jersey had to offer us in the way of a view. "She loved him, didn't she?"

"No. She sure didn't do that," I said and laughed, and then so did Janie after a minute.

"Well, what?" she asked. We had come down now to the intersection of the New Jersey Turnpike and the Pennsylvania Turnpike. From here we had to drive west almost two hundred miles before turning south again.

"They were just bound together, is all I know," I said. "I can't put any name on it. It was a lot more hate than it was love. It was pretty sad, really," I said.

Janie shook her head. "No, it wasn't," she said, and she reached for my hand, but I wouldn't let her have it, I pulled away.

"You don't know," I told her. Janie looked out her side window, and so I looked out of mine, too.

We passed through miles and miles of silence, and then Janie said, "But what if he had gone with them? What if they'd asked him, and what if Grandmama had said it was all right with her, and what if he'd said it was just what he had always wanted to do, go and live with his grandson and his grandson's wife and children?"

"It was a stupid idea," I told her. "They knew it. That's why they never asked him."

"But they were serious about it when they talked with us. They might have asked him."

"He would have said no."

"But Reed, what if?"

"Jesus Christ, Janie, I don't know. I guess they'd have made a pet out of him. They'd have fed him and cleaned up after him, and in return for that, they'd have expected him to tell Burt and Jennie amusing little stories at bedtime. They'd have trotted out their housebroken little grandparent when company came, and they'd have had him perform his routines, telling about the old days and so on. That's what people do to each other!" I was shouting at her, and I was almost as horrified at myself as I could see she was, with her wide eyes staring at me.

"Duncan and Eleanor are not like that," Janie said.

"People are like that," I said.

"No."

"*I* am like that," I said, "and I have no reason to think that anybody I know is any different from me."

"I am not like that," Janie said, softly, evenly, "and you aren't either. Shithead."

In Harrisonburg we stopped at Janie's parents' house and had coffee and a sandwich with her mother. Her father wasn't home from work, and we didn't have time to wait for him. Evelyn was proud of her newly remodeled kitchen, and we sat in there under the bright light with cheerful colors all around us. Evelyn asked me to tell her what I knew, but all I could tell her was about the phone call I'd gotten from Mother that morning after Janie'd already gone down to catch the subway for work. My grandmother had found my grandfather in the bathroom that morning. As far as they could tell, he'd died suddenly. My mother, on the phone, meaning to be kind to me in telling me about it, had sounded businesslike and almost cheerful. I'd hated that tone, had wanted to shout at her, "Well, is he dead or not?" and had been glad when the conversation was finished.

It was dark when we headed down the Valley of Virginia, the old Lee Highway now converted into four lanes of Interstate 81 that let us glide past Staunton, Lexington, Roanoke, Christiansburg, Pulaski, without slowing down, without even seeing more than a few lights from any one of those towns. Even though we were driving south at better than seventy miles an hour, the temperature was falling as we went, and I kept imagining the shrill wind outside the car as it might have been if it could strike my forehead, freeze it, numb it, turn it white with cold.

While I was parking the car in front of the funeral home in Madison, I knew that the shadow I saw on the front porch was Duncan, out there for God knew what reason, because he'd gotten fed up with everybody indoors I supposed. And when we went up there on the porch with him, I was glad to see him, found myself smiling at him, even though it didn't seem like a smile was what ought to be hanging on my face for the occasion. "Hello, Reed, my friend," he said when we shook hands. Janie gave him a big hug, Duncan patting her on the back like she needed burping, and I heard her say, "I'm sorry, Duncan." Duncan said, "I am, too, Janie girl, I am too." We went inside.

My mother was very steady. I could see that she had called up all of her strength, so that it seemed that the whole room, full of family, her relatives and my father's, and close friends, was connected directly to her. People stood or sat facing her, as if they wanted to be able to see her if she gave any signal. My father stood near her. He shook my hand, grinned at me, his public smile that was almost an expression of pain, and he was so tired that I wondered how much longer he could stay on his feet like that. Grandmama was sitting down in one of the straight chairs the funeral-home people had lined up in rows for us as if we were some kind of an audience. Grandmama had on powder and lipstick and one of the three or four dresses she owned that wasn't an old white nurse's uniform. She was in an intense conversation with her sister, Aunt Delores, and she seemed full of energy, brightly glad to see Janie and me, holding both our hands at the same time while she spoke to us.

Janie and I made our way through uncles and aunts and people I had known all my life, some of them meeting Janie for the first time. Every conversation was fractured, inadequate, so that I began to feel drops of sweat trickling down my rib cage. But after a while we were there at the far side of the crowd of them, and there was nothing to do except walk up to the open coffin where my grandfather was lying.

He looked only approximately like himself. But then I had never really seen him asleep that I could remember. I stared at his face, and I felt Janie squeezing my hand hard, but I didn't seem to be able to respond to the moment. I stared at him, waiting for something that wasn't forthcoming. Then I could feel Janie wanting to go, wanting me to go with her, and we moved back away into the crowd of family and friends, now sifting out toward the outdoors. Janie and I were the last ones to get there, through the last door and into the cold air out on the porch.

Coming down the steps from the white-columned verandah

of the funeral home, I felt like skipping or jumping around. I caught Duncan's eye over at my parents' car, where he was holding the door for my mother, and I saw that he felt it, too. A grin came across his face even though he was trying to hold it back. I tried to jostle Janie in the old friendly way we had, but from the stiffness of her body I knew she was still thinking about what we'd just seen.

Duncan drove my parents in their car, and we were supposed to follow them, Eleanor riding with us. But when she started to get in the back seat with the dog, she backed out. "Preacher had an accident," she said.

"Damn him," I said. "He always does that. He gets carsick." I went back there and cleaned it up as best I could.

Then I saw that Eleanor had gone to stand beside Janie, had put her arm around Janie, and so I said, "We might as well all three ride in the front seat." It irked me that Janie was crying like that in front of Eleanor. I would have told her to stop it, just to stop it, but she'd have had an ally in Eleanor, and I didn't feel like arguing with the two women.

In the car Eleanor said, "You know, if that's the kind of thing you have to put up with, you might as well have a kid."

"Between a kid and an animal," I said, "I'll take an animal every time." I thought that would shut Eleanor up, but she just laughed at me and said, "Oh, Reed."

Down the street from the funeral home, Duncan had pulled over my parents' car to wait for us. We followed him out of Madison, and when we were on the highway heading down to Fort Ellis, I asked Eleanor, "What do you know about how he died?"

She said that she had gotten the whole story from my mother that afternoon. "Do you really want to hear it?" she asked.

"No," said Janie, her voice muffled, as if she were speaking from inside her coat.

"Yes," I said.

Eleanor scooted over against the window, away from us, sighing.

"I want to hear it," I said.

Eleanor said that she would tell me when we got home, but I told her that I wanted to hear it now. Then Janie spoke up and told Eleanor that she wanted her to tell it now, too.

"He's my grandfather," I said, and I didn't tell them what they knew I meant, that neither of them was related to the old man at all, except by marriage. I had a right to hear how he died. They weren't blood kin.

I drove for a long while without any of us saying anything. The two women seemed to be receding from me, Janie huddled down into her coat in the middle and Eleanor gazing out the side window at the dark side of the road. Even the dog had found a place to lie down in the back seat, out of sight. I considered how the green dashboard light must make me appear to Janie and Eleanor, and I leaned over a little to see my own face in the rear-view mirror. The light wouldn't follow me, and I caught only the shadow of my head.

"He got up around five, they think," Eleanor said, all of a sudden. "Your grandmother was used to his getting up at that hour of the morning."

"In his long johns, I guess," I said.

"I don't know, they didn't say." Eleanor went on quickly, not wanting me to interrupt her anymore. "She said she went back to sleep the way she always does, and it was about six-thirty before she was aware that he hadn't come back to bed. She called out for him a couple of times, and then she got up to go see about him. She said that even then she wasn't too worried, because a couple of mornings he'd gone ahead and put on his clothes and gone downstairs because he couldn't get back to sleep. She didn't turn on any lights—"

"Too cheap to turn on any lights," I said under my breath, but they didn't pay any attention to me.

"But when she got to the bathroom, even though she couldn't see him and even though he wouldn't answer her, your grandmother said she knew he was in there. When she did turn the light on, she saw he'd fallen over toward the bathtub. His head and shoulders were back up between the wall and the bathtub. So she couldn't really see enough of him to know what was wrong with him."

Janie made a sound that both Eleanor and I heard, and we drove on for a while in silence. Then Eleanor asked softly if she should go on.

"Yes," I said, "let's get it over with."

"Janie?" Eleanor asked, but Janie didn't move or say a word. So Eleanor took a deep breath and went on with it.

"She says she doesn't know how long she worked at trying to get him out of there. She thinks she might have blacked out a while or something. She took his pulse, but she didn't know if she felt a heartbeat or not. Finally she went downstairs and called your parents. Your mother says that was around seven-thirty."

"Jesus, that's almost an hour after she found him," I said. "I wonder what happened in all that time."

"Your mother says that your grandmother was exhausted by the time they got there, about a quarter till eight. She thinks your grandmother must have pulled at him for most of that hour and maybe she did black out or go into a trance or something. Anyway it took your father another forty-five minutes to get him out of there. He had wedged himself in there between the bathtub and the wall really tightly when he'd fallen."

"I wonder if the old man would have lived if they'd gotten to him right away," I said.

"Your mother thinks he died almost instantly. She says that's the only good thing that she can think of out of the whole business. She says it was pretty terrible for all of them, trying to get him out of there."

"I'll bet it was a while before he died," I said. "That 'died instantly' stuff is just the kind of notion Mother gets when she wishes something were true that she knows isn't."

Eleanor didn't go on after that, and Janie kept quiet. "So what else is there to say?" I asked them as we turned up the hill toward our driveway, but they wouldn't talk. I was glad when I pulled up in front of our house. Eleanor and Janie went inside, murmuring to each other, and I stood outside to let the dog take his run. He disappeared in the shadows and reappeared when he dashed across a patch of light thrown down on the grass from a dining-room window. I saw a light come on in the room upstairs where Janie and I would sleep, and I saw Janie's shadow moving up there, but I couldn't see her. I considered calling out to her, waving, dancing around for her on the lawn, doing something to amuse her, but the window was closed, and I would have had to shout for her to hear me. I opened the door for the dog to go in the house, and then I went back to the car for our suitcase and our hanging bag. I was surprised to find the downstairs of the house empty. Even Duncan had gone upstairs to bed, and I had counted on talking with him a while. It wasn't even midnight yet, and they were all acting like a bunch of invalids.

I made a lot of noise hauling the suitcase and the hanging bag upstairs and turning the lights off behind me. I heard my mother call out goodnight to me when I passed her and my father's door. I answered her and waited a moment to see if she'd say anything more. Then I walked on into Janie's and my room. My high-school diploma, band pictures, a J.V. football letter, and a Beta Club sign were all hanging on the walls in there to make it officially my room, but when I was a child this had been the guest room. I hadn't ever slept here while I was growing up, and it seemed to me now, whenever Janie and I came home, as if we were sleeping in the guest room. Janie was in bed, turned with her head away from the light, which she'd left on for me. I made a show of setting the suitcase down, finding space in the closet for the hanging bag.

"You sleeping in your underwear?" I asked her, meaning to tease but sounding, I knew, as if I disapproved of her.

"Your mother lent me a nightgown," she said. She kept her head turned the other way.

"Jesus Christ," I said. "You mean I have to sleep with my mother's nightgown?" I thought I was sounding pretty funny then.

"Well, you can sleep downstairs on the couch if you want to," Janie said.

I laughed to let her know that I was kidding, but she didn't say anything, didn't move in the bed. I undressed, shivering in the cold of the room, and climbed in beside her. There was an issue of *Better Homes and Gardens* left by my mother for Janie on the bedside table. I picked it up to leaf through it. I didn't feel like going to sleep. "Did you see Grandmama?" I asked, but I didn't wait for Janie to answer. "She was talking up a storm with Aunt Delores, just like it was a social occasion. She finally got what she wanted. She's been after that old man to die for the last twenty years. I bet she can hardly wait to get him in the ground."

Janie churned up in bed beside me, and I had never seen her look at me or at anybody like that, never even imagined it. "Reed Bryant," she said, "can you shut your stupid mouth?"

I tried to meet her stare, but I couldn't, and so I turned the pages of the magazine and looked at the pictures of pie and jello salad and fondue sets. When Janie lay back down again, I kept turning the pages, but I didn't say anything else. And when I was sick of the magazine, I put it down and turned off the light.

In the morning my father still looked tired. At the breakfast table Duncan and I chattered back and forth, a very nervous but funny conversation in my opinion. Duncan did his imitation of talking with a mouthful of snuff. My mother gave him a hard look, and Eleanor whispered to him to be quiet. Janie gave no response at all to Duncan or me, and I did my best to stifle my giggling at Duncan.

He and I went outside and took turns throwing a stick for the dog. It was a bright, windy, cold day, but it was not uncomfortable for us so long as we kept moving. We talked in short, high-pitched bursts of speech, as if the cold wind would freeze our teeth if we said too much all at once. Duncan wanted to know what Janie and I would do when I finished school in New York.

"Go farther north," I told him. "Boston, Maine, Montreal, Quebec. Farther the better."

Duncan laughed. "We'll track you down," he said. "We'll follow you wherever you go." Then he asked me when Janie and I were going to start a family.

"Got a family right here," I said. "Family's chasing a stick this morning."

"Children, you dolt," he said.

I threw the stick as far down the lawn as I could fling it, and the dog looked as if he would separate himself from his own body in his frantic chasing after it.

"No children," I said. "Where are yours now, by the way?"

"With Eleanor's parents. Already I miss them," Duncan said, and he made a mock-sad face.

"Looks to me like you're having a fine time," I said.

"Wait till you get yours. Just wait," he said.

"I'm not getting any," I told him.

"Cold nights up there in the north," Duncan said. "Long winters."

"How I like it," I told him.

My father and mother rode with my grandmother in a funeral-home limousine. Duncan and Eleanor rode with Janie and me, following the black Cadillac out our driveway and down the town side of the hill to the Methodist church. Duncan and I were pallbearers, along with uncles and cousins we had not seen for years. We carried the casket from the hearse to a small metal stand at the door of the church. Then my grandfather was rolled forward into a place he had set foot in maybe two or three times in his life.

The service was perfunctory. Elton Bryant hadn't been much of a churchgoer. The Methodist minister performed admirably, speaking and praying for my grandfather. The hymns were the old-timey ones that we had to assume my grandfather would have preferred, given that he had to hear something in that line. "Shall We Gather at the River" caused a quick wrenching in my chest, and I looked around to see if anyone else had been moved by the song, the soaring glide of a woman's voice. I could see no change in anyone's face, but I remarked that the whole church was filled, that there were people from the town standing along the sides and in back of the last seats. I caught Janie's eye in the pew behind my row of pallbearers, and she held my look, didn't smile or frown but just returned my gaze steadily.

We carried the coffin out and down the steps of the church, where there were more people standing, ones who weren't able to find room enough inside. I saw Monkey Jones out there, and he gave me a sad smile, bobbed his head as he had always done when he saw me. On the other side of the coffin I saw that Duncan was looking at Monkey, too, trying to return the sad smile but simply grimacing.

My grandfather was not heavy. I kept feeling that I should be holding up more weight. We walked easily across the church lawn to the gravesite, to a small tent, several lines of folding chairs, and a green, imitation-grass canopy spread over the mound of dirt beside the grave. We set the coffin down on a kind of elevator device over the gaping hole. The funeral home had made the place look almost pretty, had made it so that no one had to look at raw dirt or even the grave itself. People took their places out there, sitting in the chairs or standing up behind them and around them. My grandmother, not crying but with her face so pale it looked almost gray, sat between my mother and father in the first row. I walked back to where I had seen Janie, and I stood beside her for the short service.

I was behind and to one side of my father, some distance back, but I saw him take off his glasses and dab at his eyes with his handkerchief. I felt then as if something heavy had dropped from my throat down to my groin. I caught at Janie's hand. She held on to me, and I was grateful to her; I thought I might have fallen if she hadn't let me take her hand. The air around me spun and sang. I felt almost too heavy to be able to walk away from the grave and go back to our car when it was time. We went along in a crowd of people, some of them relatives, but mostly people from Rosemary. The afternoon had warmed only a little; there was still a chilly breeze in the churchyard. No one wanted to stand still and talk.

When we came to the car, Janie asked me if I was all right. She was pulling her hand away from me, and I let her go.

"I'm sorry," I told her. "Was I squeezing?"

"Some," she said, rubbing her hand. She smiled at me, though.

Turning the car around, I heard Duncan tell Eleanor in a quiet voice that he had never asked the old man enough questions. "I knew only a fraction of his life, and he'd have been happy to tell me as much of it as I wanted to hear," Duncan said.

"That's right. He would have," I said from the front seat back to them. "And he's about the only one in the family I'd have wanted to tell about my life," I said. "He'd have been willing to hear that, too."

"Well," Duncan said in a tone that I recognized as his let's-not-get-too-serious voice, "I doubt if he'd have wanted to hear that sordid tale."

"I'd have cleaned it up for him," I said. "Left out the kinky parts."

"Then you wouldn't have had anything to tell him, Reed," said Eleanor, and by the time we turned into the driveway we were all four chuckling.

Janie and I took a walk while Duncan and Eleanor fixed dinner. We went up the driveway to the ridge where you could look down and see the town. "I was glad to have all those people there," I told Janie. "It's hard to imagine how many years he would have known lots of them, or they would have known him. Forty, fifty, sixty years with some of them."

"He lived here in Rosemary, in this place, all of that time?"

"Yes, I think so," I told her.

The temperature was dropping when Janie and I got back to the porch. We were arm in arm, and we took some teasing from Duncan and Eleanor when we came indoors.

At dinner my father was able to talk at some length about my grandmother. He was concerned that she would have to live alone in that big house. We assured him that he was right to let her stay there, not to insist that she move in with him and my mother or go to a nursing home. "It might be hard for her," my mother said, "but it's what she wants. It's really the only thing she'll put up with." Duncan and I agreed with her.

"I'd sure hate to live over there alone," said Janie. And we let a long silence pass before the conversation picked up again.

Janie and I washed the dishes. Then we sat with the others in my father's study until Janie said that she was tired, she thought she would go upstairs and read a while. I followed her not very long after. While I was up there looking through the bookcase to find something to read in bed with her, she said that she was really too tired to keep the light on any longer. "All right," I said, getting in and snuggling up to her, stealing part of her warmed-up sheets, "turn it out." She did, and while the others stayed downstairs talking, we were up there in the dark, breathing into the space between us.

◆ ◆ ◆ ◆ ◆ ◆ ◆ ◆ ◆ ◆ ◆ ◆ ◆ ◆ ◆

Only the

Little Bone

This summer our county has more cases of polio than any county in the nation. You catch polio from other people. Our parents decree that my brother and cousin and I must stay inside our yard. Until further notice we can't go out, and our friends can't come to see us.

Ours is an interesting yard, maybe an acre of mowed grass, an old tennis court gone to honeysuckle, and a bushy patch of woods far below the house that we call the jungle. If you had to spend a whole summer inside a yard, this one is better than most.

On the very day of the decree, we boys become bored and restless. Theoreticians of the small group advise that three is a lousy number, two against one the given dynamic. Duncan and I pick on Ralph, or Duncan and Ralph pick on me. Ralph is our cousin from Kingsport. Duncan doesn't get picked on, but he's the one who has to answer to our mother when she gets fed up with the whining.

Which is frequently. But since she interferes with our natural method of entertainment, she's the one we look to to provide us with peaceful activities. So she buys us comic books downtown, sometimes half a dozen a day. She hates it. She was raised to think of comic books as something that trashy people buy and read. I can't go with her to see her doing it, but I can imagine her standing down there at Mrs. Elkins's store in front of the comic-book rack trying to pick out ones we haven't read yet. She has to ask for the new Batman, the new Monty Hale. She's embarrassed and a little mad about it, but what can she do? She selects carefully, because if she brings us one we've already read, we howl and mope around the house for hours.

But she has to bake them before she gives them to us. The baking removes the germs. It also stiffens them, gives them an odd smell, makes them wear out quickly. Now she has acquired some skill at it, but she burned a few in the early weeks, charred a Sears & Roebuck catalogue pretty thoroughly by giving it extra minutes in the oven for its size. The baked comic books go along with the boiled water and the almost-boiled milk that tastes like liquid aluminum.

I commence a study of June bugs, those hefty green beetles. I tie threads around their legs and let them fly in circles around me. June bugs have shiny gold bellies and a sweet, oily smell. June bugs are uncommonly healthy, stupid, hard to kill, more or less blind, harmless. If you yank the thread too hard, though, you can jerk their legs off pretty easily.

This summer we are more than usually aware of our father's working too hard, always coming home tired. After supper maybe he'll toss the baseball with us or play a couple of games of croquet. But mostly what he wants to do is sit and rest. When he is home, though, we look to him to relieve us of our circumstance, all four of us hanging around him like hungry dogs. Our mother needs him to distract Duncan and

Ralph and me, to give her a little rest, to let her go upstairs and take a nap. During certain late-afternoon and early-evening hours there is the radio, the Lone Ranger, Sky King, Jack Benny, Amos and Andy.

When we catch lightning bugs and when our parents aren't looking, we crush them and smear them on our hands, then make weird gestures at each other. More fun than lightning bugs is throwing brooms up in the air trying to hit bats. There are lots of bats swooping all around our yard of an evening, and Duncan claims to have hit one once with a broom. I doubt he did, but I have to admit it is deeply pleasurable to pitch brooms up into the air with the hope of knocking down a bat. Ah Lord, one can collapse with such laughing and fall down in the cool grass and gaze up at the first stars of the night sky.

Our mother is frazzled. Our grandmother comes to visit, to help. The situation is charged. Our grandmother is a small woman, mild-mannered for the most part, but a formidable Methodist. Our mother is also uncompromising in her Methodism. These two, mother and daughter, are temperamental and likely to fall out with each other. Anger and righteousness are directly linked in Methodist ladies of my mother's and grandmother's sort. If they become angry, it is because someone else has done wrong, and they relent only if the other admits the wrong and swears to change. On other occasions of my grandmother's visiting us, she and my mother have quarreled and taken to not speaking to each other. Nights, after we boys were supposed to be asleep, we have heard the two of them carrying on their argument by speaking through my father: "If she thinks she can come into my house and tell me . . . ," and "If she thinks that's the way a daughter can speak to her own . . ."

Our grandmother is good for canasta, the one card game,

apparently, the god of Methodists must figure is O.K. Duncan and Ralph and I adore canasta, the huge hands, the double deck, the "melding" all over the table, the frequent occasions for clowning around, trying to get a laugh out of our stone-faced grandmother. Our grandmother is also good for Cokes. She drinks two a day, one at ten-thirty and another at a little after three in the afternoon. We boys usually don't get Cokes, but when our grandmother is there we get two a day. In the afternoon, we use our Cokes to make what in our family we call "foolishness," ice cream in a big glass with Coke poured over it.

But our grandmother is not accustomed to such intense exposure to my brother and cousin and me. On her other visits, our presence has been balanced by our absence: we go down the hill to Gilmer Hyatt's house to seine in the Rosemary branch for crawfish and minnows, or out to our grandfather's (our father's father's) farm to pester the men who work for him. This summer we are around her all the time, and our grandmother is more and more reluctant to accept our invitations to play canasta. She is more and more often in the guest room upstairs with the door closed.

Ralph and I sometimes sense Duncan sliding away from us. Sometimes he isn't laughing when we are. Sometimes we'll head outdoors, to the jungle, the trapeze, or somewhere, and Duncan won't be with us. He takes to spending time alone in his laboratory, the old back room upstairs where he put his chemistry set and a lot of junk that he said he didn't want Ralph and me getting into and ruining. Our mother tells Ralph and me that when Duncan is back there and doesn't want to be bothered, we are to leave him alone.

Ralph is homesick for Kingsport, but he can't go home because his mother is sick. He begins a series of temper tantrums, one a day, sometimes two. He blows himself up, gets red in the face, screams, breaks something that's handy if he's serious. I notice, though, that he chooses pretty carefully what he breaks.

I go into my pious phase. When Ralph does a tantrum, I counter with a lengthy speech about how they put people like him in reform schools and as soon as they get old enough they transfer them to prison. People who act like that. I tell him God's bad opinion of people who bust up their cousin's Army Command Post that he worked so hard to make out of glued-together used popsickle sticks from the trashcan at school. When grownups are around, I try to carry myself with dignity, to speak with unusual wisdom for somebody my age.

I have noticed qualities of my voice that are remarkably similar to certain qualities of the voice of Roy Rogers, namely a certain tenor, lyrical sweetness and also the ring of rectitude. In seeing the films of Roy and in reading his comic books, I have sensed a special link between him and me. We share the same taste in holsters, saddles, hats, boots, and shirts. For Christmas I received an orange and white Roy Rogers neckerchief that I cherish as the outward and visible sign of my kinship with Roy. Wearing the scarf is what I do when I have other things on my mind, but my preferred use of it is to run with it in my hand, trailing it in the wind behind me. I wish only that I could see it better. When the wind catches that scarf, I know that I am in the presence of beauty.

In mid-August Mother hears that no new cases of polio have been reported for the month. She tells each one of us when we come downstairs for breakfast. She keeps explaining to us until we demonstrate to her that we are happy. Even our grandmother is cheerful. We decide to take a ride to Elmo's Creek to celebrate the end of the polio epidemic.

What should be very familiar landscape for my brother and cousin and me today is so new and vivid in the warm August sunlight that we are more or less quiet going out of our driveway and down the hill to the highway and then turning toward town. My mother drives slowly, chatting with my grandmother in the front seat. She asks my grandmother to keep an eye on Duncan and Ralph and me in the back seat because she can't really turn around, she has a crick in her neck. The slowness with which we travel on the highway out of town seems to me appropriate for the occasion, a decorous speed for three boys who haven't been out of their yard all summer and their mother and grandmother. Cars pass us honking their horns, but not one of us finds that trashy behavior worth remarking.

At the creek itself of course we boys must ask my mother if we can't go swimming. We whine just enough to let her know that we would in fact go into the water if she agreed to let us, but of course we all know she won't since we brought no bathing suits and since we all know how Elmo's Creek, with its bottom full of rusted beer cans, must be swarming with polio germs. Her denial is full of good cheer. We turn around and head back home.

Vanity is not the moving force behind all that follows. On the contrary, I am wholly without awareness of self, am without sorrow or desire, nostalgia or greed, am in that state of pure, thoughtless spirit that I later come to understand as aesthetic experience, as I hold my Roy Rogers neckerchief out the car window and watch it fly gorgeously in the wind. I have had to bargain with Ralph for the place beside the door, and I have had to exercise considerable discretion in sticking my hand and arm out the window. My mother's stiff neck prevents her from turning to see what I am doing, and I am sitting behind my grandmother, whose sense of well-being is directly proportional to the stillness of her grandsons. Even Duncan and Ralph, who are inclined to sabotage any pleasure I might be taking by myself, sit quietly regarding me and the neckerchief; I think of them, too, as being under the powerful influence of art.

Then the scarf slips loose from my fingers and flies back behind the car, curling in the wind, lightly coiling down to the gray asphalt. I am too stunned to speak, and anyway I have my whole head out the window now, looking back at what I have lost, but Duncan and Ralph speak up for me, cry out for my mother to stop the car, explaining to her what has happened. She does stop. She isn't able to turn completely around in the seat, but she sits and listens to my brother and my cousin and agrees that I can get out of the car to run back along the road and retrieve my neckerchief.

In the gravel and stubble I run along beside the highway, thinking that my neckerchief is much farther away than I would have imagined it and is strangely still there in the road after having been so lively when I held it in my hand. The day is hot and bright. The fields of Mr. John Watts's farm stretch out on both sides of the highway; even though Mr. Watts hung himself in his bedroom several years ago, the land is still farmed by his kinspeople. When I reach the scarf and hold it again in my hand, I am not comforted, as I had imagined I would be. I stand on a curving slope, a gentle slope but one that seems to be pulling me away back toward the creek, away from my parents' car that has begun slowly backing down the incline toward me but that seems such a distance from me that it will be long minutes before I can climb into the back seat with Duncan and Ralph and we can resume our stately homeward ride.

At the top of the hill another car appears, the sun flashing on its chrome grille and bumper. At a fair speed it heads down toward my family's car, which my mother has maneuvered into the middle of the highway in her effort to back up to me. I am concerned that there will be a collision, and I sense myself standing on the roadside, first on one foot and then the other. The strange car, a black sedan, doesn't slow down as it approaches our car. I can see the dilemma the driver faces, which way around my mother's middle-of-the-road-backing-up-vehicle he should take. He chooses the side that sends him directly toward me, not slowing and, once he has aimed himself toward me, not veering to left or right. Wanting to move but not being able to make my feet step in any direction, I stand on the side of the road, aware of raising my hands as if to ward off a pillow thrown by Duncan or Ralph. I catch a glimpse through the car's windshield of a Negro woman's face, looking directly at me, her mouth open and shouting something I can't hear. Then the car brushes me, I spin and fall and see the car sail over the fence into Mr. John Watts's alfalfa field.

I am surprised at what has transpired, intensely interested in the car in the field, all the doors of which are now opening, with Negro men and women climbing out and looking back at me on the roadside. Then my mother is there, so grimly calm that I barely recognize her. She wants to know if I am all right, and I tell her that I am. She tries to help me up, but I find that one of my legs won't hold me. It doesn't hurt—I tell her that, too—but I prefer sitting down in the road. She gathers me into her arms.

A Negro man with a kind face helps Mother carry me to the front seat of our car. He winces whenever he looks into my face, and so I tell him that I am all right, I just can't stand up. Someone brings me my neckerchief. My mother and the Negro man speak to each other with enormous civility. His name is Charlie Sales. He is from Slabtown. He will stay there with his car until the police come. My mother will take me to Dr. Pope's office back in town. The car door shuts. She holds me. People look in at us through the windows. My grandmother, in the driver's seat, says she can't drive our car, then puts it into low gear and drives it all the way to Dr. Pope's office.

The small bone of my left leg is cracked. At the Pulaski Hospital they pull a stretch-sock over my whole leg, then they wrap that with wet plaster-of-Paris bandages; the bandages are warm, and the hands wrapping them around my leg and smoothing out the plaster of Paris are comforting to me. My toes stick out, and a nurse holds them while the others work. I don't sleep well in the hospital that night, but my mother is there in the room with me to murmur to me in the dark, bring me water, put her cool hand on my forehead.

Charlie Sales had no brakes in that car. He feels terrible about what happened. My parents take no action against him; our families have known vaguely of each other for years. My mother takes her share of the blame for the accident because of her car being in the middle of the road because she was backing up but she had that crick in her neck so that she couldn't really see straight. When people ask her about the nigger that was driving the car that hit me, she says it wasn't Mr. Sales's fault. When they see my mother's attitude, they don't call Mr. Sales a nigger anymore. In the family, though, my mother wants it understood that it is her magnanimity that is saving Charlie Sales from being put in jail and losing every cent he has. Our family generally tries to do good in the world, but among ourselves we want credit for our excellence. Whenever anybody says that name, Charlie Sales, I see not him but that woman's face looking at me through the windshield, her mouth open, saying or shouting something I can't hear. Maybe she is Mrs. Sales. I don't know. When I imagine the accident again, it is graceful. The car brushes me, almost gently, and I spin a turn or a half a turn and fall. The car breaks the top strand of barbed wire on the fence when it sails into the field.

When I go home I have to stay in bed a week or two, and then I can ride in a wheelchair with a contraption that sticks out for me to rest my leg on. The cast is heavy for me, and someone must help me lift it when I move. The wheelchair is an old-fashioned wood-and-metal apparatus that is unwieldy in our house. I am always knocking into furniture or walls or something. I quickly learn that I won't be disciplined by my parents and that Duncan or Ralph are reluctant to do anything to me in my wounded state. I continue to think of myself as benign and heroical, in the mode of Roy Rogers during the few days he sometimes spends with his arm in a sling. But when Duncan and Ralph are home I follow them in my wheelchair from one room to another, insisting that they play with me.

One day I throw my cap pistol at Duncan. I miss him, but our grandmother sees me do it. She wants me to be spanked. I can see her point, but I'm glad my mother won't do it and won't let her do it. The righteous anger of the Methodists sets in on both sides. They don't speak. The grandmother demands to be taken home. My father agrees to take her after the air show we've planned to attend in Pulaski on Saturday.

My mother and grandmother don't want us boys to know they are quarreling, and so they try to act as if the condition of their not speaking to each other and the grandmother's barely speaking to me while being warmly solicitous of Duncan and Ralph is the normal condition for us all to be in. We three boys pretend we know nothing, but we eavesdrop on all their conversations, which can take place only when my father is there. Our spirits can't help but be dampened in the presence of the adults, who sigh and gaze out the windows at mealtime. Ralph, trying to relieve the social anguish of one suppertime, slouches down in his chair to allow his mouth to come to plate level, and he scrapes the food in. Duncan and I find that pretty funny and register our amusement with sly grins. Our mother, however, sees the grins and sees the source of them, reaches over and whacks Ralph lightly on top of the head so that his face plops into his plate. Ralph looks up with bits of corn sticking to his face. All of us laugh, and for a moment the old family pleasure is there among us. Then our grandmother excuses herself but goes to sit only as far away as the living room. Solemnity comes quickly down again.

It rains at the air show. Many of the acts are canceled, others are invisible, though an announcer describes them to us through a static-crackling P.A. sytem. There is a parachutist who comes down close enough to our car to make us boys not want to leave the show. But mostly we sit in the car in a field full of other cars, and our grandmother and mother both cry, sitting beside each other in the front seat while my father tries to make himself invisible with his hat down over his eyes. We boys whine to get out of the car into the rain and whine for refreshments and whack and pinch each other, writhing in our state of misery and hilarity. Duncan and Ralph must be wary of my leg in the cast. I have the advantage over them.

You'd think things would improve immediately with the grandmother gone, but they don't. For one thing, Duncan has taken to exercising what he sees as his "adult privileges." Eating breakfast one morning, he calls our mother by her first name, and she throws the empty dish-drainer at him. For another thing, I become so impossible in my behavior and demands that it does become necessary for my mother to spank me. This is very hard on her. And finally, I become much more mobile. My cast has gradually lightened its pull on my leg. Sitting on my butt, I can scoot up and down the steps without assistance. And my grandfather has made crutches for me. These are sturdy crutches, just the right size, probably made with the help of three or four of his men. I am delighted with them and launch myself around the house on them.

And take a fall immediately. And continue falling several times a day, great splatting, knocking-into-furniture-and-breaking-things falls that cause everyone in the family to come running to me, my mother frequently in tears. My grandfather has forgotten to put rubber tips on the ends of my crutches. When we figure this out and buy the rubber tips and put them on the crutches, I stop falling. But by then the bone-set that was coming along nicely has slipped, and the doctor has ordered me back to the wheelchair for another several weeks, has ordered the cast kept on for an additional month or five weeks.

The missing crutch-tips are the first clue I have to this peculiar family trait, one that for lack of any better term I must call "flawed competence." We Bryants are a family of able and clever people, industrious, intelligent, determined, and of good will. We are careful in our work. Remember, my grandfather measured me on two occasions before he made the crutches. But we usually do something wrong.

Four years later I become increasingly aware of "flawed competence" when I develop a plan for converting our old grown-over tennis court into a basketball court. My grandfather is always interested in plans, and in this planning session, we decide that he will make the hoops, and he will help me make the backboards. Clearing the ground and smoothing the surface will be my tasks. So I rip out honeysuckle and hatchet down a few little scrub cedars, working a couple of hours a day after school for a week. It becomes clear to me that there is at least ten times more work to be done here than I had in mind originally, but I hold fast to my plan and continue the work. We Bryants are known for setting our minds to things.

Then my grandfather delivers the hoops. They are beautifully designed and constructed, metalwork of a high order for such amateurs as my grandfather and his men, who are mostly talkers, cursers, storytellers, spitters, and braggers. But the hoops are twice as big around as ordinary basketball hoops.

I say, simply, that they are too big. I am not ungrateful, not trying to be hateful, not in my opinion being overly fastidious. I am simply describing a characteristic of the hoops. But my grandfather's feelings are damaged. No, they can't be made smaller, and no, he's not interested in helping me with the backboards now or with any other part of my plan. He's sorry he got involved in the first place. This, too, is a corollary of "flawed competence." We are sensitive, especially about our work, especially about the flawed part of our work.

At the place where I work twenty-eight years after the basketball hoops, I am given a new office, a corner one with two large windows and a view of the lake. There's a string attached, though, and that is that I have to build my own bookcases. I commence planning with enthusiasm. That's another, less harmful family trait, that attraction to making plans. I measure, I look at other people's shelves, I get a guy to help me attach brackets to my office walls.

It is while I am cutting a notch in one of the uprights to allow access to the light-switch by the door that I suddenly think of my grandfather and those basketball hoops. I feel a light sweat break out on my forehead. A pattern of genetic fate reveals itself to me: I'm going to gum up these bookshelves just as my grandfather before me would have gummed them up. This very idea I'm working on, the notch in the upright for the light-switch, is a Granddaddy Bryant kind of idea. No doubt I'm sawing the notch in the wrong place. This epiphany comes to me at night in my new office with a fluorescent ceiling light shining down on me and my reflections from both windows mocking me full-length while I stand there with the saw in my hand.

The whole time I work I wait to see where the screw-up is going to come. I imagine what my colleagues will be saying about me in the hallways. Did you know that Bryant built his shelves so they tilt? Did you know that Bryant's books rejected the color he painted his shelves? But the screw-up doesn't appear. I paint the shelves red, and they look O.K. (Granddaddy Bryant once painted yellow a whole row of company houses he built.) I paint a rocking chair blue and red, and it's a little silly-looking, but it picks up the blue of the carpet and the red of the shelves. The vision isn't nearly as impressive as I thought it would be, but then what vision ever is? We plan-makers are accustomed to things turning out not-quite-as-good-as-what-we-had-in-mind. Our *Weltanschauung* includes the "diminished excellence" component. Diminished excellence is a condition of the world and therefore never an occasion for sorrow, whereas flawed competence comes out of character and therefore is frequently the reason for the bowed head, the furrowed brow. Three months later, when I try to turn the heat off in my office, I discover that I have placed one of the shelf uprights too close to the radiator to be able to work the valve. The screw-up was there all along, but in this case I am relieved to find it. I am my grandfather's grandson after all.

In the spring, on a visit to my parents' home, I am out in the toolshop behind the garage. Up in the rafters I find those old basketball hoops. Since I have so recently thought about them, I take them down and stand for a moment weighing them, one in each hand. My grandfather has been dead for twelve years now, and I have this moment of perfect empathy with the old man: the thing he worked on so as to be part of

my life was no good; when I told him, "They're too big," I
pushed him that much further away from me and that much
closer to his own death. Those old hoops are monuments to
something. They're indestructible, and perfectly useless. God
knows what some archeologists of the future will make of
them when they dig them up out of the rubble.

Stashing the hoops back up in the rafters, I find this other
thing, too, the cast from my broken leg. When the doctor
sawed it off, somebody taped together the two parts and gave
the thing to us to take home. It is a child's leg, slightly bent
at the knee, grayish-white, not much larger than my arm. It
is at one and the same time utterly strange and utterly familiar.
The little bone of my leg was broken one day because I'd
dropped my Roy Rogers scarf out the car window when we
were taking a ride to Elmo's Creek to celebrate the end of
the polio epidemic the summer we had to stay inside the yard
and my mother couldn't back up straight because she had a
crick in her neck, and so Charlie Sales, whose car had no
brakes, had to swerve and miss her and therefore hit me.
Holding that cast in my hands, I can almost understand the
wacky logic of that accident.

That light, hollow little leg that is somehow my own calls
up layer after layer of memory in me. Both my mother and
my grandmother have softened their tempers, have taken on
that Methodist sweetness that you feel in hymns like "Bringing
in the Sheaves" and "A Walk in the Garden." Whatever
wrongs that grandmother might have committed, she has been
harshly dealt with, first with glaucoma and then with a skin
cancer that works on her slowly. I doubt she even remembers
the day of the rained-out air show when she and my mother
wept in the front seat while my father pulled his hat down
over his eyes and Duncan and Ralph and I writhed in the
back seat.

My mother still remembers when Charlie Sales hit me,

still holds herself responsible, still takes on a sober expression and a sad voice when she speaks of that day. And once at a party in New York, I met a black woman who spoke to me of people she was related to, Saleses from Madison County, Virginia. That seemed so significant to me. I told her the story about Charlie Sales hitting me with his car and breaking my leg. I told the story in such a way as to make it seem all my fault and my mother's, Charlie having to choose which one of us to hit. I thought the story would make an incredible impression on this dignified black woman. I thought she would acknowledge our deep and lasting kinship. I still remember her face—serene, interested, kind, polite. Yes, she said, it was probably her kin-people who came piling out of that car, she said, she didn't know for sure, she hadn't been back there since she was a child. And she turned away from me to talk with someone else. But, in my memory, her face became the face of the woman I saw in the front seat of Charlie Sales's car, just before it touched the little bone in my leg. Memory and fact are old cousins yammering away about whether or not there even was a strand of barbed wire on that fence for the car to snap when it flew into the field and how could I have seen it anyway, having just been knocked and spun around by the car.

I stand there holding that cast in my hands, reading something somebody in my third-grade class wrote on the side of the knee, and I know that everything that happens is connected to everything else and nothing that happens is without consequence. I am washed by one memory after another like ripples moving backwards to their source. All of a sudden I am no one. Or I am this stranger standing in an old toolshop with memory trying in its quirky way to instruct him. A man came home to visit his parents, a man who got an office and built bookshelves, a man whose grandfather died and who was a soldier for a little while, a boy whose leg was broken by a car and who did not become a basketball or a football player, a boy who stayed a summer with his brother and his cousin inside his family's yard. The moment of my disappearance passes, and I come back to myself. Now, holding this cast in my hand, standing just in this one place, I feel like I could remember all of human history. If I put my mind to it.

The Mirror Experience (hike)

ONLY THE LITTLE BONE

has been set in a film version of Electra by Crane Typesetting of Barnstable, Massachusetts. Designed by William Addison Dwiggins for the Mergenthaler Linotype Company and first made available in 1935, Electra is impossible to classify as either "modern" or "old-style." Not based on any historical model or reflecting any particular period or style, it is notable for its clean and elegant lines, its lack of contrast between the thick and thin elements that characterizes most modern faces, and its freedom from all idiosyncrasies that catch the eye and interfere with reading.

The book was designed by Virginia Evans. It has been printed and bound by Haddon Craftsmen, Scranton, Pennsylvania.